Jessica Fren[...] writes[...] [...] [...] is repressing so[...]thing. I feel that as a[...] not telling me everything that happened on the day his brother disappeared. I have no concrete reason for feeling this way. I cannot say that he has been evasive, either in what he has written or said, verbally or in his demeanor. He is a very open child and I believe that he would find it quite difficult to knowingly lie. That, perhaps, goes to the heart of my intuition that he is not sharing with me all that his memory holds about his brother's disappearance. I believe it is possible that something traumatic happened to him on the day in question and that he has repressed it. I realize that this does not constitute a revelation, as the possibility of something traumatic happening (i.e., that his father, Dr. Miles Gale, was responsible for Aaron's disappearance) is precisely the reason C.J. is being held in a foster home until this whole bizarre and tragic situation is resolved."

Also by T.M. Wright in Gollancz Horror

T.M.

WRIGHT

LITTLE
BOY LOST

VGSF

First Gollancz Horror edition published 1993
by Victor Gollancz
An imprint of Cassell
Villiers House, 41/47 Strand, London WC2N 5JE

A catalogue record for this book is available
from the British Library

ISBN 0 575 05026 8

Printed and bound in Great Britain
by Cox & Wyman Ltd, Reading

For my friend and agent,
Howard Morhaim

LITTLE BOY
LOST

ONE

My dad said this was a good idea. He thinks I'm a pretty smart kid. That's what he says all the time, anyway, that I'm a smart kid, and that I notice things that most other people don't.

"I asked him what he thought you wanted me to say, and he said what you said, that you wanted me to *remember*. 'So remember everything, C.J.,' he said. 'Remember colors, noises, movement,' he said. That was pretty confusing. There are so many colors and noises and movements, everywhere you go. The blue sky, the green grass, the wind blowing the grass, the calls of birds, the noise of kids playing, people swearing, all that stuff.

"But I said I'd try and remember and he seemed glad. 'It's very, very important, C.J.,' he said, and I knew that it was. I know that what happened to us isn't something that happens every day.

"And I want to get Aaron back, too, just like Dad does. And like you too. But I think Aaron is gone forever. I don't think we'll ever find him, even if we go back to the place where we lost him.

"Because I think the universe is a really scary and topsy-turvy place, and you can't count on it to do what you expect it to. Most of the time it will. You drop a glass of milk and it goes *crack* on the floor and the milk spills all over. But I think that, one time out of a billion, or a trillion, that glass of milk won't go *crack* against the floor and make a big mess. One time out of a billion, it'll do something else. Maybe it'll hang in the air for a long, long time, or maybe it'll turn into a fork right in the middle of falling and you'll look down and see the fork on the floor and you'll think, *Where is my glass of milk, and how did I get two forks, anyway?* Or maybe it'll float down like a soap bubble. Who knows what it'll do exactly? But it won't do what it's *supposed* to do, because the universe is such a topsy-turvy place, like I said, and we really shouldn't depend on it doing what we think it's going to do. And that's important, Dr. French. I think that's *real* important!" He paused dramatically to punctuate what he'd just said, then he continued, "And that's why Aaron's gone. Somebody reached out and took him and we'll never get him back because now he's in a place that no one can get to.

"I told Dad all this, and he said that maybe I was right, maybe we won't get Aaron back, but we've got to try. He says that people think we're crazy, too. Him especially."

C.J. stopped talking. The sudden silence took Dr. Jessica French by surprise. She leaned forward over her desk, clasped her hands on the desktop, and conjured up a friendly, authoritarian smile. "Is that what you think, C.J.? That your father is crazy?"

C.J. tilted his head, bemused. He was a good-looking eleven-year-old, green-eyed, pale-complexioned and quick to grin. He grinned now. "You'd know that better than *I* would, Dr. French," he said. "Do *you* think we're crazy?"

"What I think, C.J., is that we have a situation that requires attention—"

"You *don't* think we're crazy?"

"Actually, C.J., 'crazy' is a word we try not to use very much. It's really not a very descriptive word, is it? It doesn't tell us anything—it's more an epithet than—"

"What's that?"

"You mean 'epithet'?"

C.J. nodded. "Yeah."

"Well, it's a name you might call someone. Like a swear-word. For instance, some people use epithets against black people. They call black people, like me, bad names. Do you understand?"

C.J. shrugged. "Sure, I guess."

Jessica nodded. "Of course you do." She indicated the four cassette tapes that C.J. had brought with him into the office, the result of a week's worth of nearly constant re-cording (this was Thanksgiving week, and C.J. had had the last five days off from school; he wasn't due to go back for another three days).

"Could I please see those now?" Jessica asked.

C.J.—the initials stood for Christopher Jonathan—handed the tapes across the desk to Jessica. "I've been working real hard on 'em. I've never talked into a tape recorder like that so much before. I don't need to, and I don't need to write anything down either, because I remember everything."

Jessica nodded. "Yes, I know."

"But it all just sort of . . . came out. And I couldn't stop it." He grinned. "And I just kept on talking. That's why there's so much of it."

Jessica grinned back, said, "I understand," and asked if it was all right with C.J. if she began listening to the first tape immediately, while he was in the room. "That way," she explained, "if you feel the need to clarify something—" She paused; did he want her to tell him what "clarify" meant? Apparently not. She went on, "Then you can jump in. Okay?"

He nodded. "Okay," he said, and Dr. French put the first tape, marked "1," into a small Sony tape recorder on her desk and hit the PLAY button. C.J.'s voice came over the little speaker almost immediately; there was no "Testing, testing," no hesitation:

WHAT HAPPENED THE DAY
AARON GOT LOST

"I was in the front seat, Aaron was in the backseat, Dad was driving. We were going to Triphammer Mall. Dad needed to buy something for his girlfriend because it was her birthday. She was thirty-one. Dad is thirty-eight. He keeps telling everyone that he's thirty-five, but he's only joking. He jokes a lot.

"Dad's girlfriend's name is Lorraine Rabkin and she is always laughing and telling jokes, too. She's a lot of fun, and very pretty, too, with long red hair and a pretty face, and she's very tall, almost as tall as my dad, who is six feet two, and when she smiles she's so nice to look at that it makes me feel funny and fluttery inside. Dad likes her a lot. Her and Dad are always smooching in front of us. It's kind of dumb, but it's okay, I guess.

"My dad is an archaeologist. He works at the university, sometimes he teaches, and sometimes he does research and what he calls 'fieldwork.' 'Early American People,' which is what he calls them, are what he likes to work the best with. People who lived here in America, around where we live, thousands and thousands and thousands of years ago.

"Lorraine wasn't with us in the car, of course. It was *her* birthday present we were going to be getting, after all. It was only me in the car and Dad and Aaron, who was in the backseat reading a comic book, *Masters of the Universe.* Dad hates *Masters of the Universe* and I do too. I think it's too violent, which is what Dad thinks. But Aaron likes *Masters of the Universe* because he's only six years old and he doesn't know any better and he likes the violence.

"He started reading the comic book when we left the house. It's only a little ways from the house to Triphammer Mall. Five minutes. We stopped on the way to get the car washed. There was a car ahead of us, and it was a green and white 1977 Chevrolet Malibu and its license number was ITB-276. This car went through the car wash pretty fast. Then we went through. Then we went to the mall. I think Aaron was probably still reading his comic book when the back door to the car opened and I turned around and I saw that he wasn't there anymore. Wherever he went to, he took that comic book with him."

Jessica stopped the tape. "What can you tell me about your brother?" she asked.

"Huh?" C.J. said.

Jessica smiled pleasantly. "Do you like him?"

It seemed a very odd question to C.J. Who wouldn't like his own brother (half brother, whatever)? "Sure," C.J. said. "I like him."

"And you get along well?"

"You mean do we fight?"

Jessica shook her head. "No. I realize that all siblings fight now and then. I mean, do you play together? Are you friends?"

Another odd question. Who in the heck could be friends

with their brother? Brothers were *brothers! Friends* were friends. Friends weren't related to you. "Huh?" C.J. said.

Jessica could see that the boy simply didn't understand what she was asking. She tried another approach. "If Aaron wasn't your brother, and he was your age, do you think that you'd play with him? Would he be your friend?"

C.J. thought about this for a moment. *Another* odd question, but at least he could answer it. "I guess so," he said.

"You seem uncertain," Jessica said.

"Uncertain?"

"About whether you'd be Aaron's friend or not."

"If he wasn't my brother, you mean?"

She nodded.

"Well, I guess he's kinda weird."

"In what way?"

C.J. shrugged. "I don't know. He says weird stuff all the time. About his mother—"

"Marie?"

"Uh-huh. And about people."

"What people?"

"People people. He says, 'Those people.' And I say to him, 'What people?' And he says, 'Those people I see,' and I say, 'What people? When?' And he says, 'When I'm asleep. And other times, too.' That's what he says. 'And other times, too.' And he doesn't tell me what other times."

Jessica sat back in her chair and gave C.J. a curious look. He stared back expectantly. At last, Jessica asked, "And what about his behavior?"

"I dunno," C.J. answered. "He fights a lot. He likes to fight. And hit. He's got a real violent streak in him. My father always talks to him about it, and so does Lorraine. But it doesn't do any good."

"Who does he fight with? Kids at school?"

C.J. nodded. "Uh-huh. There are a couple of bullies and they used to pick on him, but he broke one of their noses so they don't pick on him anymore." C.J. smiled, then fought the smile back, obviously uneasy with the fact that he liked what he was saying. "And there are some other kids, too. Kids who call him names."

"What sorts of names?"

"Oh, 'weirdo,' stuff like that. Which is what he is, really. A weirdo, I mean. So you can't blame the kids. But he beats them up. He hits them with his fists. He knocks them down. He's really big and strong for a six-year-old. My dad says it's because Marie was so strong." He fell quiet; his mood grew dark, suddenly.

Jessica said, "Is something wrong, C.J.?"

He shook his head a little.

"Something about Marie?" Jessica asked.

He didn't answer.

"Was *she* weird?"

He said nothing for a moment, then nodded earnestly.

Jessica said, "Marie was weird?"

He nodded again. "Weird as shit!"

"And how weird is that, C.J.? What exactly did she do that made her weird as shit?"

C.J. looked quietly at her for a couple of moments. Then he said, "Can we talk about something else?"

TWO

Miles Gale remembered that he'd rolled his window down because he couldn't stand the new car smell that permeated the Chevy's interior. He remembered, too, that he had been intent upon putting the car into park (it was equipped with a floor-mounted stick shift that he still hadn't gotten the hang of), and upon turning the radio off (so it wouldn't blast him when he got back into the car and turned the ignition on). Consequently, his gaze was on the area of the stick shift, the ignition, the radio's on/off button (*Everything is buttons,* he remembered thinking, nostalgic for the days when car radios came with easy to use, utilitarian knobs), and he remembered hearing something very strange, considering where he was—in a parking spot at the Triphammer Mall, seven acres of trendy specialty shops surrounded by ten acres of asphalt.

He remembered hearing leaves rustling in a sudden brisk wind.

But there were no trees here. There were trees around the perimeter of the parking lot, a thousand feet away, and they were bare because it was late November.

He looked.

He saw tall pine trees jutting into the sky. Maples, oaks,

tulip trees, heavy with summer foliage, grandly swaying in a stiff wind.

"My God!" he whispered.

He heard the rear door—Aaron's door—open, close.

Then the trees were gone and he saw storefronts, people walking, a dog running loose.

He turned his head, looked at his son, C.J., sitting in the passenger's seat. "Did you see that, C.J.?" he asked.

C.J.'s eyes were wide. "Aaron's gone!" he said.

WHAT HAPPENED THE DAY AARON GOT LOST

"The dog was not very big and he had long gray fur around his nose that made him look like a little old man.

"He looked scared, too, maybe because he was in such a noisy place and there were so many people and so many cars.

"He wore a red collar around his neck, and there was a silver tag hanging from it. Every few moments he looked this way and that like he was lost. I felt sorry for him. I had been watching him since we got to the parking lot and Dad started looking for a place to park. Once, I turned around and I said to Aaron, 'Look at that dog, Aaron, he might get hit or something.' But Aaron was reading his dumb *Masters of the Universe* comic book and he didn't hear me, I think.

"But Dad said, 'The poor thing looks frightened.'

"And I said, 'Yeah. He looks frightened.'

"The dog was in the parking lot, then, when I first saw him. He was running between cars. Not really running, more like tripping along, like he wasn't really sure which direction he wanted to go every time he took a step.

"I saw the trees then, when I saw the dog for the first time. I didn't tell Dad because I saw them only for a second and they were like ghost trees, trees you could see through, because I could see the mall through them. I thought it was a very strange thing to see, even for a second. I haven't ever seen anything like that before and I didn't think that I was just imagining it, even for a moment. I still don't think I was imagining it. The trees were real, and I could see through them.

"Dad said, 'Is something wrong, C.J.?' and I remembered that I gasped or something when I saw the trees, and that's why he asked if something was wrong. I shook my head and I looked back at Aaron and asked him, 'Did you see that, Aaron?' But he was still reading his dumb comic book, his *Masters of the Universe* comic book, and he didn't hear me.

"I looked at the dashboard clock on Dad's new car. I don't know why I looked at it, I just did. I think that I was hoping Dad would turn the radio down, a song called *Rainy Day Women* by Bob Dylan was playing and I don't like Bob Dylan's voice much, it's whiny and raspy at the same time, and the dashboard clock said 2:14. It's a digital clock. Dad explained what digital was. Numbers instead of dials. He said that it was a way of making everybody tense, having them look at a number for the time instead of a dial for the time. He said, 'You're seeing only the moment, not the whole sweep of the day. You're not seeing *time,*' but I wasn't really sure what he meant, and he's always talking about things like that anyway, things I don't really understand."

Dr. Jessica French stopped the tape and looked at C.J. He was sitting up straight in the ladderback chair in front of her desk. His pale, handsome face was blank, his hands were folded in his lap, and he was wearing a neatly pressed, white long-sleeved shirt, a pair of black pants with a razor-edged crease, and very bright white tennis sneakers. Jessica thought that the white shirt did not suit him because of his pale complexion—he looked like an apparition.

Jessica said, "Do you like your father, C.J.?"

He looked nervously at her. Another odd question. Why wouldn't he like his own father? "Yeah. I like him."

"You get along with him, then?"

C.J. shrugged. "Sure. Why not?"

"Does he punish you?"

"Punish me for what?"

"For anything? For lying, for instance, or for not picking up after yourself. Things like that."

C.J. shook his head earnestly. "Nope. Because I don't lie, and I always pick up after myself."

Jessica sighed. "Then your father never has occasion to punish you?"

"He hollers sometimes."

"He gets angry, you mean?"

"Uh-huh. But everyone gets angry. Don't *you* get angry, Dr. French?"

"From time to time, yes."

"And don't you yell, or throw things, or hit?"

"Is that what your father does when he gets angry? He hits?"

C.J. stared intently at her for a moment. She was baiting him, he realized. "My father *never* hit me, Dr. French."

"And he never hit your brother, either?"

"Nope."

"Not once?"

"He slapped him on the ass a couple of times."

"Hard?"

"Hard enough to make him cry."

"Why did he do that? Do you remember, C.J.?"

"I remember, sure. It was a couple years ago, but I remember."

"Do you want to tell me about it?"

"It wasn't anything important. I mean, it wasn't anything interesting. Aaron was just actin' up, that's all. He was being a little brat, like he does a lot. He was trying to fight with my father and my father had to slap him a couple times on the ass, and then he didn't want to fight anymore."

"Aaron was actually *fighting* with your father? How old was Aaron, then? Was he four years old?"

C.J. nodded. "Yeah. Four. Almost five. It was February fifth, and his birthday is February thirteenth, and he was fighting with my father because he didn't know who my father was, I think; he was talking like he didn't know who my father was. He was saying things like 'All of you, get away,' like my father was more than one person, you know, and he was hitting my father with his fists, so my father whipped him around and slapped his bottom a couple of times, and that's when Aaron stopped fighting with him."

"I see," Jessica said. "And that was the only time he hit your brother that you can remember?"

"Sure. There wasn't any other time that I can remember."

Jessica looked at him a moment, then asked, "You have a photographic memory, isn't that right?" She knew well enough about C.J.'s photographic memory; she wanted to see how he felt about it.

C.J. nodded glumly. "I remember everything. Even stuff I don't want to remember."

"Oh. What sort of stuff do you mean?"

C.J. shrugged; he looked very uncomfortable. "Like stuff from when Dad was married to Marie."

"Aaron's mother?"

"Yes." He nodded. "He married her a year and three days after my mother . . . died."

"I see." Jessica didn't like making C.J. remember his mother's murder, but there was a disappearance under investigation—the *second* disappearance involving a member of the Gale family in the past eighteen months. "Could you tell me what you don't like to remember about Marie?"

Again C.J. shrugged. Then he scowled. "Lots of stuff."

"What sort of stuff? Could you tell me something in particular?"

C.J. looked suddenly angry. "You think that my dad did something awful to Aaron and that he made up the story about Aaron disappearing out of the car just to cover it up, don't you?"

"Is that what your father told you? That we suspect him of doing something awful to Aaron?"

C.J. shook his head.

"Then what makes you ask me that question?"

C.J. sighed again. The ghost of a nervous smile played on his lips and was gone. "Because no one," he said, "is going to believe that Aaron was just . . . snatched out of the car like that. That's a crazy thing to believe."

"But you said that it really happened, C.J. Are you telling the truth?"

He nodded sullenly.

"You looked back from the front seat and Aaron was just gone?"

C.J. nodded again. "He was gone. He wasn't there anymore. One second he was there, then he wasn't there."

"And you heard the door open and close? Did you look back when you heard that?"

"No."

"Why not?"

"I *told* you!" He was angry again. "Because I saw those trees. I was scared because I saw those trees"—he was whining now—"and I didn't remember that I heard the door open and close until later on, when me and Dad were home and he was talking to me about what happened." He was close to tears.

Jessica got up, came around the desk, got down on her haunches and put her hands on the boy's slim shoulders. "Would you like to go home now, C.J.?"

"Will my dad be there?"

Jessica sighed. "For the moment, as you know, we think it's best if you stay with the Podkomiters. You like them, don't you?"

C.J. said, "You want me to stay with the Podkomiters because you think my dad's going to do something to *me,* too!"

Lorraine Rabkin, standing in the doorway between Miles Gale's kitchen and living room, said, "There's one bottle of Coke left. Want to share it?" She held the bottle of Coke up for him to see. She attempted a lighthearted grin.

It had been two weeks and a day since Aaron's disappearance and barely twenty-four hours since C.J. had been taken from him to live, until the investigation was completed, in a foster home.

Miles shook his head. He wasn't looking at her. He was looking at a display of family snapshots above the fireplace. "No. Thanks," he said. He looked at her. "My God, I miss them," he said. "I miss my kids so much, Lorraine—I feel like I'm going to explode."

"I understand that, Miles. I miss them, too."

She turned, went into the kitchen, put the bottle of Coke

back in the refrigerator, went back to the doorway. Miles was still looking at the display of snapshots. Some of them showed his second wife, Marie.

Lorraine said, "I'm with you on this, Miles. I love you."

Carl Podkomiter nodded at C.J. Gale, who was being walked up to the Podkomiters' front porch by a policeman. Carl, who had been away from the house on business and had not yet been introduced to C.J., said, "So, he's supposed to be real smart, huh?"

His wife, Irene—blond, thin, with a broad, flat face that bore an almost constant look of annoyance—said, "He's got a photographic memory, Carl. I don't know if that means he's real smart."

"What else could it mean? If he remembers everything, then he's got to be real smart, right?"

Irene shrugged. "Sure. I guess."

Carl Podkomiter said, "He's probably great at Trivial Pursuit."

C.J. and the policeman arrived at the base of the front porch. Carl and Irene smiled. "Hello, again, young man," Irene said, and came down the steps and took C.J.'s hand. Irene said to the policeman, "We'll take it from here, Officer."

He nodded, said, "Yes Ma'am," and went back to his patrol car.

WHAT HAPPENED THE DAY
AARON GOT LOST

"Dad's car is a brand-new Chevrolet Celebrity Eurosport
and he likes it a lot, and just before we went to Triphammer
Mall, we went and got it washed. All of us stayed in the car
while it went through the car wash. The spray of water and
suds on the windows was like being in a really big thunder-
storm and Aaron even looked up from his dumb comic
book and said, 'Oh, wow!'

"Dad paid $2.50 to a man named Dave when the car
wash was through. It only took a minute to get the car wash
done, and then we went straight to the mall.

"I didn't see the little black dog there right away. I saw
two people who were pushing a grocery cart full of pop
bottles. These people were a man and a woman and they
were dressed in blue jeans and the woman had a red and
white print blouse on and the man a T-shirt with the words
Shit Happens on it.

"I also saw someone who looked like Marie. She is the
woman that Dad married after my mom died, and a year
and a half ago she went out to get some groceries and never
came back. This woman who looked like Marie was standing in front of a restaurant called Sledge's, which was a long
way away. I didn't see her face very well, but the woman
had long black hair down to her waist, like Marie, and she
was wearing a blue dress that ended at her ankles, and she
was standing very still, the way Marie used to. I said to
Dad, 'Look at that woman, Dad. She looks like Marie,' but
he didn't look because he was trying to find a parking space
and the parking lot was pretty crowded.

"Then the woman was gone because a green car went in

front of her, and right after that is when I saw the little black dog again, and since I knew that the woman couldn't be Marie, I got interested in the little dog and hoping a car wouldn't hit him.

"The sky was cloudy and it was sort of warm. Dad had the window rolled down because of the smell in the car. 'New car smell. Some people like it, I don't,' he said, but it was all right, it wasn't too cold."

"Gone?" Miles remembered saying. "What do you mean Aaron is gone?" Then he looked into the backseat, where Aaron had been sitting. It was empty. He remembered the door opening, closing. "Dammit!" he whispered. Aaron had gotten out of the car by himself, without waiting for him—Miles—to tell him it was all right, there were no cars coming. "Dammit!" he whispered again, and looked out his driver's window.

No Aaron.

He looked right, left. Still no Aaron.

He started to get worried; he wasn't sure why. Surely Aaron was within shouting distance. He couldn't have simply vanished.

"Aaron!" Miles shouted. He opened his door and got out of the car. "Aaron, where are you?"

There were a number of people nearby. They looked over; some of them looked about, as if they might be able to spot Aaron.

WHAT HAPPENED THE DAY
AARON GOT LOST

"After Dad got out of the car, I got out, and I went around to where Dad was standing.

" 'Aaron, where are you?' Dad called. I saw three people look at him. Two old people who were walking together, and a woman. The woman was carrying a baby on her back in one of those baby carriers. The baby carrier was blue. The baby was asleep. The word *Perego* was printed on the baby carrier in red. The woman wore green pants and a gray jacket that was puffy at the shoulders—"

Dr. Jessica French hit the tape recorder's STOP button and sighed. A photograhic memory, like C.J. Gale's, must surely be a burden. All this essentially useless information bouncing around in his head. Jessica wondered if, as the child grew older, he'd be able to discriminate between what information was important and what wasn't, or if his head would always be a warehouse for worthless facts—words printed on T-shirts, colors of strangers' jackets, license plate numbers, et cetera. A pity, too, that the child hadn't more innate intelligence. He seemed above average, certainly; testing could tell Jessica exactly how bright C.J. was, although she didn't see any real reason for it. But, if he were exceptionally gifted (and it was obvious that he wasn't), then he would probably be better able to integrate and make use of all the facts that day-to-day living would throw at him. As it was, a lot of people would probably think of him as a genius, simply because of his ability to rattle off facts his amazing memory had absorbed. And that—the unreasonably high expectations of other average people—would be a burden on him, too.

C.J. Gale had a hell of a life ahead of him.

Correction. He had a hell of a life *behind* him. Mother is murdered when C.J.'s not even five years old. Father remarries a year later, and his new wife—whom C.J. apparently despised—goes out one night for chips'n'dip and a six-pack of Sprite and never returns. Then his half brother, Aaron, son of his father's second wife, turns up missing a year and a half after that.

No, C.J. Gale's eleven years of life had not been filled with good times and sunshine.

Jessica turned the tape recorder on again.

THREE

Last Friday, about two-fifteen," Detective Hugh Vinikoff said. He was middle-aged, chunky, almost constantly tired, and looked it.

The clerk at Sledge's Restaurant nodded. He was tall, young, painfully thin; his face sported a week's growth of blond beard and, because his skin was ruddy, the contrast made him look like an albino. He said, "I was here. I saw all the cop cars."

Detective Vinikoff said, "Did you see anything else?"

The boy shook his head at once. "No. I don't remember nothin'."

"Nothing at all?"

"What am I supposed to remember?"

"And you didn't *hear* anything, either?"

"I heard the sirens."

"I mean before that."

The boy shook his head a little, clearly uncertain. He shrugged, bony shoulders rising and falling like the shoulders of a marionette. "I don't know. Some guy shouting."

"What was he shouting?"

The boy thought a moment. "I don't remember. I just knew that somebody was shouting. I couldn't hear *what* he was shouting, exactly. Someone's name, maybe."

"Short name, long name?"

"Huh?"

"What did it *sound* like?"

"Sound like? I don't know. It sounded like . . . *Urp!*"

Vinikoff sighed. *"Urp!* Is that supposed to be funny?"

The clerk shook his head earnestly. "No. I wasn't trying to be funny. That's what it sounded like. *Urp!* You can't really hear much through that glass." He indicated the big windows that looked out on the parking lot.

"Of course," Detective Vinikoff said wearily. "I understand." He glanced out the windows. The parking lot was full; there was a constant stream of traffic—people looking for parking spaces—but he could hear very little except a continuous low humming noise, as if a hive of bees were trapped in the floor beneath him. He looked at the clerk again. "And you didn't actually *see* anyone shouting?"

The clerk shook his head. His broad smile had vanished. "No. I don't think so."

A man in a booth nearby shouted, "Hey, can we get some more coffee here?"

FOUR

Miles Gale said, "They think I . . . did something to him, Lorraine. They think I did something to my own son." He closed his eyes, felt his face flush with emotion. "To my own son, for Christ's sake!"

Lorraine reached across the table, where they were having a light lunch, put her hand over his and gripped it hard, in reassurance. She wanted to say something comforting, but could think of nothing that hadn't already been said. He would understand her silence, she knew. That was the essence of their relationship—understanding.

Miles sighed and shook his head in disbelief. "He just *wasn't there anymore,* Lorraine. I looked back and he wasn't there. And I looked . . . we looked, C.J. and me, we looked in that damned parking lot and in the mall for hours. And he *wasn't there.*" A pause. Miles shook his head again. "He wasn't *any*where." He raised his hand—the one Lorraine had been holding—and brought it down hard on the tabletop, causing his full glass of milk to slosh over onto the table. "Dammit!"

Lorraine flinched.

Miles stood abruptly and went and looked out the little, multipaned window above the sink; it showed him a curving line of new "high aspect homes"—one spiral arm of the

Towering Pines subdivision that his home was part of. But there were no pines, only a couple dozen young maple trees that had been trucked in by the developer, stuck in the middle of each house's front lawn and held in place with wire and white tape.

"They could have kept some of the pines, anyway," he said, as if to himself. He turned his head and looked angrily at Lorraine. "They could have kept some of the damned pine trees! How in the hell can they call this place 'Towering Pines' when there aren't any damned pine trees? They're doing the same thing everywhere you look. 'Poplar Ridge'—no poplars. 'Sunny Brook Estates,' and there's no brook."

Lorraine looked back silently. He was ranting; he was entitled.

He looked out the little window again. "I despise this place. I don't know why the hell I moved here. The boys. It was for the boys. I thought it would be safe. I guess it is. I guess it's safe. But I despise it."

"The police will find Aaron," Lorraine said.

Miles said nothing.

Lorraine added, "You don't believe that, do you?"

He shook his head without turning to look at her. "You know who's going to find Aaron?" he said at the window. "Not the police. Not the people who are looking for him." He thumped his chest with his fist. *"I'm* going to find him." He turned his head and looked at her, green eyes ablaze. *"I'm* going to find him, Lorraine. I can *feel* it!"

WHAT HAPPENED THE DAY
AARON GOT LOST

"And Dad was saying that he wished he had a cigarette. 'I wish I had a damned cigarette,' he said. That was when me and him were looking in the parking lot for Aaron and not having much luck.

"I said to him, 'Cigarettes are bad for you, Dad. Besides, I thought you quit.'

"And he said, 'Go look over there. Keep calling to him.' And he pointed at the front of a J.C. Penney's store.

"Then a man came up to us and asked, 'Are you looking for someone?' The man was one of the Mall Security Police, and his name, which was written in red on his brown uniform shirt pocket, was Fred Armstrong. He was a tall man, and a little bit overweight, too. His face was round and his forehead was very high and his eyes were blue and looked gentle. I thought when I saw him that he would make a great Santa Claus and I pictured him in a Santa Claus suit.

"And my dad said, 'I lost my son.' He held his hand up to just above his own waist and said, 'He's six years old, about this tall. He's got brown hair and brown eyes, and he's thin.'

"Fred Armstrong asked, 'How long ago?' and my dad answered, 'Maybe five minutes,' and he pointed and said, 'We're parked over there.'

"A plane went over real low, then. It was a big plane, a passenger plane, and when it went over it made lots of noise.

"Fred Armstrong asked, 'Could you tell me your son's name, please?'

"And my dad said, 'Aaron.'

"Fred Armstrong said, 'And what's he wearing?'

"And Dad answered, 'He's wearing Osh Kosh blue jeans and a yellow long-sleeved shirt. And a white jacket.'

"A woman in a green dress went by. This woman was old. She was probably sixty, and she was walking very stiffly and carrying a J.C. Penney's box that had a red ribbon around it. A present, I think. The woman had three rings on one hand. One of the rings was blue . . ."

Jessica French sighed. For a while, C.J. had been on sort of a roll, not straying too much from the point, and now he was going on and on about this woman carrying a J.C. Penney's box and wearing three rings.

Jessica fast-forwarded the tape for a few seconds, stopped it, pressed the PLAY button. More talk about the woman with the J.C. Penney's bag. The color and style of her shoes and hair; her changes of expression as she walked past and looked at Miles Gale and the security guard talking, et cetera, et cetera. C.J.'s preoccupation with this woman was understandable, Jessica thought. His father had told him to remember *everything,* and that's precisely what he was doing. And it was easy to see how the woman might have interested C.J.—an outsider peering in at the heartbreaking drama unfolding. It would be nice, though, if she—Jessica—could do some judicious editing as she listened, otherwise she'd be at this until the wee hours. She glanced at the clock on her desk; it read 10:45. There were still three ninety-minute tapes to listen to, and this one was not even half finished.

"C.J. says that he saw Marie there," Miles Gale said to Lorraine. "At the mall. When we pulled into the parking area."

Lorraine said nothing.

Miles shook his head. "No, I don't think C.J. actually saw her. I think he saw someone he thought *looked* like her—"

"How many women look like Marie?" Lorraine asked. It was a good question. "She was pretty much one of a kind."

Miles nodded. He had a cup of freshly poured coffee in hand and he sipped it delicately. "Ow," he whispered, because it burned his tongue. "Yes," he said, "she was very much one of a kind. But C.J. saw this woman from a long way off. It could have been anyone. And I'm positive it wasn't Marie."

"Why?"

He gave her a quick, incredulous look. Then he said, "Because I think that Marie is long gone. If you split . . . if you leave someone, you don't hang around the place you left them. At least, Marie wouldn't. And *that* I'm positive of."

Lorraine said, "She was my friend before she was your wife, Miles. I think I knew her at least as well as you—"

"Oh, come on."

"You doubt it?"

"Doubt it? No. I just think it's not true. You couldn't have known her as well as I. The relationship was a lot different, worlds different—"

"We were very close, Miles."

"I don't think anyone got 'very close' to Marie. She let you think so, but I don't think it was possible to get genuinely close to her. Hell, she proved that by running away, by leaving me *and* her only child."

Lorraine thought about this. Remarkably, she had never looked upon Marie's disappearance in that light. She had seen it only as the bizarre resolution of a dispute between her—Marie's—life-style and Miles's life-style. In some ways, Marie was a very traditional woman. She liked order and ritual in her life; she had her own personal rituals, in fact. She said prayers before the mundane events of the day—prayers before sleep, prayers before meals, prayers before leaving the house, even prayers, she had confessed to Lorraine, before lovemaking.

The prayers she said were not traditional, it was true. They didn't appeal to a loving and tempestuous God for guidance and protection. They were songs to the earth, to the sky, to the seasons. They were part of her Indian heritage, she explained, and she was inextricably bound up with them.

Miles, on the other hand, was a man who gave little to chance or to things unseen. In most things, he was a pragmatist. He had no rituals. And he had made it clear more than once that Marie's rituals made him uncomfortable.

Lorraine said, "I don't think that she left Aaron for good. At least"—she sighed in sad recognition of the events of the past fifteen days—"that wasn't her intention."

WHAT HAPPENED THE DAY AARON GOT LOST

"There were trees and they were all around. They were northern white pine, and spruce and hemlock, maple, tulip tree, too.

"The trees were so tall and there were so many of them that the forest was dark, like it was almost night.

"And I whispered to him, because I was very afraid, and I didn't know what might be listening, or who, 'It's the woods, Dad.'

"But I don't think that he heard me."

FIVE

Detective Vinikoff—his large head supported by his hands—stared blankly into the big bowl of Manhattan clam chowder and wondered if Miles Gale was a murderer. Vinikoff did most of his best thinking while he was looking at food. Reflective food, like this clam chowder, worked best because he could see himself in it, could see the overhead lights, the room he was in, so he got a smeary picture of his temporary place in the world and he could make that picture into a point of focus. Looking into reflective food was something like reciting a mantra. It helped conceptualize things as they were and, without conscious effort, to put them together into something sensible. This was true thinking—to form a kind of transitory wisdom of complex things as they were, of the things in the world. Now, for instance, Miles Gale. Aaron Gale. C.J. Gale. Missing children and missing and murdered wives, and stories of trees sprouting up in shopping mall parking lots, and then disappearing. These were the things of a complex and mystifying world.

He continued staring into his big bowl of Manhattan clam chowder and at last let the idea come to him that Miles Gale might be a murderer, but that his son, C.J., told a remarkably detailed, if unbelievable story.

Why would C.J. lie?

"Is there something wrong with the chowder?" a female voice said above him.

Vinikoff did not turn to look. "I'm meditating," he said. "I'm sure the food is quite palatable."

"Yes, sir."

He waited for the sound of footsteps to signal that the waitress had gone away. No footsteps. He said, gaze still on the reflective red surface of the chowder, "It's all right. Everything's all right."

"Yes, sir."

Again he waited for footsteps. There were none. Reluctantly, he looked up. The waitress was thin, dark-haired, her face was pointed. She said, "We're going to be closing in a minute, sir. Actually, we're closed now, if you don't mind."

He stared blankly at her. At last, her words sunk in. "Closed," he said, merely in echo of what she'd said.

"Yes, sir. But please feel free to finish your meal." She nodded and smiled at the chowder.

He hesitated, then tasted some of it. It was cold, bland. He made a face, stood, fished a five-dollar bill from his wallet and handed it to the waitress. "Keep the change," he said, and started to leave.

"Actually, sir," the waitress called, "the bill was seven-fifty."

He looked back. The waitress was holding his check out to him. "Seven-fifty for clam chowder?" he asked incredulously.

"And salad, too," she said. "Plus milk and coffee."

Lorraine Rabkin said, "They didn't believe you?"

"Of course they didn't," said Miles Gale. "How could they?"

A brief silence in the darkened bedroom. "Yes, I suppose you're right."

"Do *you* believe me, Lorraine?"

"I believe you saw something. Yes."

"You don't believe I saw what I said I saw?"

Another brief silence. "No."

"C.J. saw it, too."

"I realize that." Lorraine rolled to her side, put her arm over Miles's chest. "I think you both saw something. But I don't think it had anything to do with Aaron's disappearance."

"I don't either," Miles said.

There was a knock at the front door. Probably in recognition of the hour—11:30—it was a soft knock, but it was also oddly insistent.

Miles lurched when he heard it.

"Who could that be?" Lorraine asked.

"I'll go and find out," Miles said.

WHAT HAPPENED THE DAY
AARON GOT LOST

"We all had tuna fish sandwiches on whole wheat bread and milk and Fudge Sundae ice cream for dessert before we went to Triphammer Mall to buy Lorraine a birthday present.

"Aaron didn't eat all his sandwich. He never eats all his sandwich. He's not a good eater, which is contrary to the way little kids are, I think. The little kids in school all eat whatever they can and whatever is put in front of them, unless it's vegetables of one sort and another, cruciferous vegetables especially.

"But not Aaron, who has favorite foods but they are very limited, such as cottage cheese and applesauce, which he mixes together into gross green and white lumpules, and also potatoes with mushroom gravy as long as the potatoes are mashed really fine so they're like paste. His culinary appetites"—Jessica French smiled—"are not as cultivated as they will be I am sure when he is as old as me.

"Dad told him, 'Finish your sandwich, Aaron. It's good for you,' which is something that Dad has said a zillion times and which he now says the way someone says something they don't mean much, and so Aaron didn't say anything back and didn't finish his sandwich either, and we got into Dad's new car (a Chevrolet Celebrity Eurosport that's brown and shiny and which looks very sharp, Dad says, after it's washed) and we went out to buy Lorraine Rabkin her birthday present after we ate our dessert, Fudge Sundae ice cream, which Aaron ate all of, of course."

Detective Vinikoff, standing at Miles Gale's front door, said, "I'm sorry I woke you, Dr. Gale. I wanted to ask you a few questions. If this isn't a good time, I can come back in the morning."

Lorraine, wearing a long blue velour robe, was standing just behind Miles. She looked offended by Vinikoff's arrival at so late an hour, but Miles nodded and smiled and said, "No, it's okay. Come in," and stepped aside. Lorraine stepped aside, too, though with reluctance.

Vinikoff came into the house, looked about, nodded at a green armchair. "May I sit down, please. I'm beat."

"Sure," Miles said amicably, "sit down."

Vinikoff sat heavily in the armchair, pulled a pack of Marlboro Lights from the breast pocket of his gray suit jacket, then, scowling, put the cigarettes back. "Sorry," he said. "Habit."

"Go ahead," Miles told him. "I'm sure there's an ashtray around here somewhere."

Lorraine gave Miles a questioning look. Why the hell was he being so friendly?

"No," Vinikoff said, "that's all right. I can live without them." He smiled. The smile vanished. He looked intently at Miles, who was standing close by and grinning uneasily. Miles's blue velour robe—he and Lorraine had bought the robes to match—was open a bit beneath his waist, and his red bikini underwear was visible. Lorraine noticed this. "Miles," she whispered, "you're exposed," and while Miles was pulling himself together, Vinikoff said, "Mr. Gale, I must be blunt and ask you—did you participate in the disappearance of your son?"

Miles's mouth dropped open in surprise; he closed it, shook his head. "I've . . . told you . . . all this . . . before," he stammered.

Vinikoff nodded. It was a gesture of weariness and resignation. He looked like a huge nodding gray tomcat. "I'm aware of what you've told us, Dr. Gale." His voice wheezed. Bronchitis. "I've read all of your files. Voluminous as they are. So I know what you've told us, not just about your son's disappearance, but about your second wife's disappearance, too, and about your first wife's murder. I'm simply not sure that I believe you."

"That's obvious," Lorraine said.

Miles glanced at Lorraine, then at Vinikoff again, who had once more fished his pack of Marlboro Lights from his suit pocket. He shook one of the cigarettes out and put it gingerly between his lips, as if it were something explosive.

Miles said, still grinning uneasily, "I can't help what you

don't believe, Detective. I think it's very clear . . . I mean, you didn't have to come here in the middle of the night to tell me you don't believe what I've told you. My God . . . I'm not *stupid.* You've put my son in a foster home. That tells me *something!"*

Vinikoff said, the cigarette bobbing between his lips as he spoke, "Again, I must be blunt, Dr. Gale. Things seem to *happen* around you. It's made us all very suspicious." He gave Miles a broad, toothy smile.

Miles whispered, teeth clenched, "Don't give me that goddamned Cheshire Cat smile. I *know* what you're trying to tell me, Detective. You're trying to tell me that you know something that I don't want you to know. You're trying to tell me . . . you're trying to tell me"—his tone was loud and nasty, now—"that you've got my number, that I'm not going to put anything *over* on you. Shit! Look at you. You're trying to be *Columbo,* for Christ's sake! You're too *fat* to be Columbo, Detective!"

Lorraine took Miles's hand. She had seen this behavior from him before. Amiability erupting into anger. He was entitled, certainly, but Vinikoff was probably not the wisest choice of targets for his anger. "Miles, please," she said.

Miles shook her hand away and pointed stiffly at Vinikoff. "Get up off my chair!" he barked. "Get out of my house! You have no right here, you have no right at all to come here in the middle of the night and play your stupid shitass cop games—"

Vinikoff pushed himself heavily to his feet as Miles continued to rave at him. He nodded, grinned, was clearly happy to have gotten such a visceral reaction from Miles. "I'm going, I'm going," he said, then made his way quickly to the door, and was gone.

WHAT HAPPENED THE DAY
AARON GOT LOST

"And when I saw the woman who looked like Marie I thought maybe it is Marie, and she's come back, she knows that we're here, at the mall, to shop for a birthday present for Lorraine, and she's going to surprise us, she's going to say, 'Here I am again. Hello.'

"I said to Dad, 'Look at that woman, Dad. She looks like Marie.' But he didn't hear me.

"I thought about Marie's last words to us before she went out and disappeared. That was a year and a half ago, June twelfth. Her last words were, 'I'm going out now. Don't miss me. I'll be back.' Then Dad said to her, 'Drive carefully,' which he always said. He said it to Mommy, too. I remember that very clearly, even though I was only three or two or even one at the time. Then Marie opened the door and went outside.

"When we were looking for Aaron there was a man staring at us from behind the window at Sledge's Restaurant. This was a tall man who was young and had a beard, kind of, and who watched us for a very long time. He works at Sledge's. His name is Michael."

<u>SIX</u>

C. J. Gale lay awake in the dark in his bedroom at the Podkomiters' and remembered too clearly and too well what he had seen in the moments before his half brother Aaron had disappeared.

He remembered the trees.

He remembered the soothing, startling white noise of wind pushing through the trees.

He remembered . . . remembered . . . He strained to see with the wonderfully acute eye of his memory. He saw a bird perched at the very top of an incredibly tall pine tree. A large bird. *A hawk?* he wondered. *An eagle?* Yes, an eagle. White head, broad, brown body, small, golden eyes. And in his memory, he saw that those small eyes were trained on him.

This was the first time he remembered the eagle at the top of the pine tree. It surprised him that he had not remembered it before. It was such a wonderful thing—such a grand and wonderful and scary thing. An eagle with its golden eyes trained on him.

But there were no eagles. He knew that. Not in New York State, anyway. Only a very few, the book said. A couple of them recently released to give the birds a chance to reinstate themselves. And those couple birds were somewhere else.

Troy. Pulaski. Not here. Not around the Triphammer Mall.

His bedroom door opened. A line of yellow light fell across his bed. Irene Podkomiter stuck her head into the room. C.J. looked. He saw a dark oval with a halo of blondish hair. "Asleep, dear?" the dark oval asked.

C.J. said nothing.

Irene Podkomiter stepped back and closed the door and the room was dark again.

Miles Gale was quivering. He was quivering because he had recently gotten very angry. He tried not to get angry because he didn't like the aftereffects. Quivering was one of those aftereffects. Feeling foolish was another. Civilized men did not let themselves lose their tempers the way he had.

Lorraine told him, "He deserved it, Miles."

They were seated across from each other at the kitchen table. There were heavy, white restaurant-type mugs filled with coffee in front of them, but neither Miles nor Lorraine was drinking.

"Yes," Miles agreed. "He did." He picked up his cup of coffee. His hand quivered. The coffee sloshed over the sides of the mug onto the table and he set the mug down and grimaced. "Dammit!" he muttered.

"Don't get angry at yourself," Lorraine soothed. She reached across the table and put her hand on his.

"Why not?" he blurted. "I acted like an idiot. Why shouldn't I get angry at myself? Jesus, Lorraine, I could feel it coming. The anger. Because I knew what the hell he was doing here. I *knew* what he was going to say. But I kept telling myself, *Now if you just keep smiling, everything will be all right.* I always tell myself that and I get angry, anyway. Maybe I should just . . . go with the flow."

A large black ant appeared on the edge of the table near Lorraine. It was a problem at the subdivision—carpenter ants. Various pest control companies had been brought in, traps had been set by homeowners, chemicals put down, but the ants persisted. Miles had said it was poetic justice, that a billion carpenter ants would undo in ten years what a hundred human carpenters had done in two. Lorraine flicked the ant off the table, watched it hit the wall nearby, then land in a stainless steel bowl filled with water; the bowl had been put down for the family cat. She watched the ant struggle for a few seconds, find the edge of the bowl, climb up a half inch, fall back in, then start struggling all over again. "Look," she whispered, and nodded at the stainless steel bowl.

Miles looked. "Did you do that?"

"Uh-huh. I flicked him off the table and he landed right there in the bowl."

"Really?"

"Really."

The ant's struggles grew weaker suddenly. Lorraine stood, went over and picked up the bowl, took it to the back door and tossed the water into the night.

She closed the door, ran water into the bowl, set it on the floor, then sat down again.

"Where *is* Buster?" she asked. Buster was the cat, a huge black and white Maine coon cat who bit and purred, lashed out and rubbed human ankles all with equal ease and encouragement. "I haven't seen him all night."

"Out," Miles said. "Getting lucky, I imagine." He picked up his coffee mug and noticed that his hand had stopped quivering. He was thankful for the diversion provided by the ant.

Lorraine said, "Dark out there."

"It's night," Miles said.

"Night, yes," Lorraine whispered. "Still, it's darker than you'd imagine."

"Pitch-dark?"

"Pitch-dark. Yes. Darker, really."

Miles got up, went to the back door, looked out. "No," he called to Lorraine. "Not pitch-dark. All these houses have spotlights. Didn't you notice?"

Lorraine joined him at the door. She saw the spotlights. "They weren't on before, Miles."

He looked at her. "Really?" he said. He closed the back door, put his arm around her waist. "I'm tired," he continued. "Real tired."

"Me, too," Lorraine said.

They went back to bed.

SEVEN

C. J. Gale had been nearly five and a half years old on the day of his mother's murder. He'd been talking for over four years, and for half that time had been sharing the workings of his amazing memory with anyone who'd listen.

When he was two, he said to his father, "And then the man on the TV said, 'Get the hell out of here.'

"And the other man said, 'You're talking to the wrong person, bub.'

"And the first man said, 'I know what you've been doing—' " Then, two-year-old C.J. went on to recount the entire thirty-minute TV show, including commercials ("I can't believe I ate the whole thing," he said in a monotone, and rubbed his stomach; "Scrubbing bubbles, scrubbing bubbles," he said in a similar monotone).

Now, nine years later, he could, if asked, recall that TV show with nearly the same clarity that he had recalled it then.

And, if asked, he could recall with equal clarity the events surrounding his mother's murder.

Could recall getting up and starting down the stairs and calling, "Mommy, I want Maltex for breakfast. Can I have Maltex for breakfast?"

Could recall pausing on the stairs and thinking, in so many words, *What's wrong?*

Could recall hearing his father get out of bed and go into the bathroom.

The radio in the kitchen playing classical music. Mommy liked to listen to classical music in the morning.

A big, noisy truck stopping out in front of the house (later, he would learn that this was the garbage truck making its regular Monday morning pickup).

His father leaving the bathroom; the toilet finishing a flush; his father going back into the bedroom.

The announcer on the radio saying, "That was Mozart's *Prelude in G,* Kerschel listing 112."

His father calling from the bedroom, "Jo"—his mother's name was Joanna; Jo was her nickname—"have you put the coffee on? I've got to get to school right away."

Could recall himself moving again, down the stairs, toward the kitchen, slowly.

The garbage truck grumbling off.

The radio announcer: "Coming up next, 'Morning Edition.' "

His father calling, "Jo? Coffee?"

Seeing, just inside the entrance to the kitchen, as he moved further down the stairs, his mother's red slipper on the cream-colored linoleum.

Calling again, "Mommy, can I have Maltex?" but knowing that something was wrong now. Mommy had not answered him and had not answered Daddy, either. Something was very, very wrong.

"Jo?" His father's voice. "You downstairs, Jo? Have you put the coffee on?"

"Daddy?" His own voice.

Seeing first his mother's foot, then her ankle, then her

calf. Mommy was lying down on the kitchen floor. Why was Mommy doing that?

"Mommy?" His own voice.

Pausing, again, on the stairs.

The radio announcer: "Coming up on 'Morning Edition': 'Is there life after fame?' Some people whose names were once household words say no. Also, 'Can shut-ins earn money through work-at-home schemes?' Several state attorneys general say 'Watch out!'"

"C.J.?" His father's voice just above him, on the landing. "C.J., what's wrong?"

"Mommy!"

"Jo?"

The radio announcer: "That's next, on 'Morning Edition.'"

A rain starting. Hard. Pushed by wind, so it sounds like a million pebbles hitting the big picture window.

"Jo?" His father moving past him, down the stairs.

"Jo!" His father's voice. "My God! Jo!"

The radio announcer: "Thirty minutes past the hour."

Irene Podkomiter said, "Well, *I* think he's spooky." She was lying on her back in her twin bed. Her husband, Carl, was in his twin bed beside her. They no longer slept together because Carl took all the covers and, on cold nights, Irene often woke up with a stiff neck.

"For heaven's sake, Irene, the kid's not *spooky*!" Carl objected. "He remembers everything. So what? Be a curse, if you ask me."

"It's a curse on us to have him here."

"You sound like a child," Carl told her.

"You know what he's probably doing in there? He's probably remembering everything that happened to him today; he's probably replaying the whole day over and over again. Fast speed, slow speed. Everything we said to him, everything anybody else said to him, everything he ate, everything *he* said. Spooky!"

"Go to sleep," Carl grumbled.

"I can't go to sleep. Hell, we don't need the money so much that we have to have somebody like him living with us."

"What do you mean, 'Somebody like him'? He's not a bad kid. He's polite enough. He doesn't sass us."

"Sure he's polite. But that's only a game. Inside, he's cooking something up."

"Oh, for God's sake, Irene, what could an eleven-year-old be cooking up? Go to sleep!"

"I can't go to sleep."

"You said that."

"Well, I can't."

"Then go downstairs and get yourself something to eat. It'll help you sleep."

"No it won't. It'll give me nightmares."

"It depends on what you eat, Irene. If you eat chili before you go to sleep, then you'll have nightmares. It's a proven fact. But if you eat something like . . . something that has carbohydrates, spaghetti without sauce, for instance—"

"Who eats spaghetti without sauce?"

"I mean with garlic sauce, or butter sauce. Like that. Jeez, you always give me an ar—"

A scream from C.J.'s bedroom cut his sentence off.

Lorraine Rabkin lay awake beside Miles Gale. She didn't know if Miles also was awake. She said, "That's quite a wind. Hear it?" The windows were closed, and the wind was rattling the panes, making them whine.

Miles didn't answer.

"Do you hear that wind?" Lorraine said, a little louder.

Still, Miles didn't answer.

Lorraine listened for a moment to his breathing in the dark. She grimaced. Dammit, he was asleep.

Lorraine found that she was a little frightened by the wind. It was very strong, stronger than she had heard it in a long time. She wanted to turn on the lights; that would help to dispel her fear. The wind in the dark was something fearsome. She thought she could feel its tendrils moving in the room.

"It's okay," Miles said.

She lurched. "Jesus, you startled me. I thought you were asleep."

"I was. The wind woke me."

"I've never heard it so strong."

"Maybe I should close the curtains or something."

"Why?"

"In case one of the windows breaks."

"You think the windows are going to break?"

"No."

He got out of bed. He was naked. She could see him move like a ghost to the window, his white skin softly reflecting what little light there was in the room. He closed the curtain on one window, went to the other, beside it, closed the curtain there.

He turned, faced her. The wind was still rattling the panes, still making them whine. "That's quite a wind," he said. "It's stronger than I think I've ever heard it, before."

"Come back to bed," Lorraine pleaded.

He stood quietly for a moment. "Yes," he whispered— she didn't hear him beneath the wind—and came back to bed.

She snuggled up next to him.

They listened to the wind for a long while, ambivalent about it. It was too strong to be restful. But it was amazing, too. A wind to be listened to in awe, a wind full of colors and lights.

Finally, when it subsided, they slept.

"Why did you scream, young man?" Irene Podkomiter demanded.

C.J. was sitting up in bed. The light was on. His face was alive with fear and he was shaking his head violently.

"I asked you why you screamed!" Irene prodded.

"Dream," Carl Podkomiter said; he was standing in the doorway, hands in the pockets of his checkered robe. "The boy had a bad dream."

"Well, I *know* that, you nincompoop," Irene snapped. "I *know* he had a bad dream. Young men don't scream in the middle of the night for nothing."

Carl shrugged. He wanted to be free of the discussion, wanted to be back in bed.

"What kind of dream was it?" Irene demanded of C.J.

But C.J. did not answer.

"Tell me about your dream, C.J."

C.J. stopped shaking his head.

"Tell me about your dream, C.J."

"Mom," C.J. whispered.

"I'm not your mother, dear."

C.J. glared at her.

She repeated, "I'm not your mother. Your mother's not here."

C.J. looked wide-eyed at Carl, then at Irene, again. "I don't remember," he said.

Irene grinned. It was toothy, flat, aggressive. "Of course you do, C.J. You remember *every*thing."

Carl said, "For God's sake, Irene, why can't we just go back to bed—"

"You do what you want," Irene snapped at him. "But if we don't find out why this boy screamed in the middle of the night, he's going to do it again, and again, and we are *never* going to get to sleep."

"I don't remember," C.J. repeated.

Irene stared at him for a long moment. At last, she said, "If you scream again, if you wake us up again, then we will have to punish you. Is that understood?"

C.J. said nothing.

"Is that *understood?*"

C.J. nodded. He said, "Yes, it's understood."

EIGHT

And C.J. could have remembered this, too, from several years in the past: he could have remembered his father showing C.J.'s mother, Joanna, a photograph he'd brought home from the university; the photograph showed a yellow skull lying in an inch of black earth. The skull had a jagged hole in it, just above the forehead.

C.J. could have remembered his father saying to his mother, "Jo, look at this."

And Joanna saying, "Is it significant, Miles?"

"Very. She was apparently quite an important person, judging from the artifacts we found buried with her. But she was buried outside the common burial area, and we don't understand why."

So many memories were open to C.J., so many pieces of the puzzle.

"There couldn't have been a wind last night, Lorraine," Miles Gale said. He was standing at the back door. Lorraine had offered to make breakfast.

She said, "Of course there was a wind, Miles. We heard it."

He shook his head, glanced at her. She was ladling fried eggs onto a plate. He looked out the back door again. "I don't know what we heard, but it wasn't wind. There are piles of leaves everywhere, all raked up. Nice, neat piles of leaves, just like there were yesterday."

She joined him at the back door, saw the piles of autumn leaves, said, "You're right."

"Yes," Miles said. "I know."

"Are you prepared to tell us why you woke up screaming last night?" Irene Podkomiter asked C.J. over a breakfast of sausage, pancakes, home fries, orange juice, and scrambled eggs.

C.J., who had not yet eaten—he wasn't used to such a huge breakfast; it seemed almost obscene to have so much food in front of him—glanced at Irene and shook his head. "I don't remember," he said, repeating what he had told her the night before.

"Of course you remember, darling," Irene said, grinning. "You remember *every*thing."

Carl Podkomiter, who'd made his way through four sausages, five pancakes, a generous portion of scrambled eggs, and two tall glasses of orange juice, and who was casting about for more food, said, "We know that you have a photographic memory, C.J. So you can't tell us you don't remember. It just won't wash. Pass me those sausages, Irene."

Irene passed the sausages.

C.J. said, "It was about my mother."

"Which mother, darling?" Irene asked. "The first one or the second one?"

C.J. gave her a shocked look.

"Eat your breakfast, dear," Irene said, unmindful of the look C.J. was giving her. "You can talk to us while you eat so long as you swallow first."

"I have only *one* mother!" C.J. said tightly. "I never had another mother. Marie wasn't my mother. Marie was just somebody that Dad married. She wasn't my mother!" He was shouting now, caught up in the flow of emotion, and he was leaning forward over the table.

Irene pushed him, hard, so he sat back abruptly in his chair.

She gave him another of her flat, aggressive grins. It was lopsided, very red—she was wearing bright red lipstick, which was her habit on weekend mornings—so it looked almost hideous. "I'm afraid we don't allow such behavior from children in our house, dear," she said.

"Better listen, now," Carl Podkomiter said, punctuating his words by pointing at C.J. with his fork. "Irene will sit on you if you don't listen and if you're not respectful."

Irene glanced at him, sighed, looked at C.J. again. "I didn't want to push you, darling." She seemed to mean it. "I had children of my own, you know, and I was very rarely . . . physical with them." She reached out to touch C.J.'s face—an act of contrition—but the table was too wide, so she withdrew her arm. "I didn't hurt you, did I?" she asked, but C.J. merely glared at her and said nothing.

"Eat your food now, dear," Irene said. "Eat all your food. We don't want it to go to waste."

Six Years Earlier

"You give me life," Marie says.

"That's a strange remark," Miles says.

"Only a gesture of thanks."

"For what?" Miles says.

"For giving me life."

WHAT HAPPENED THE DAY
AARON GOT LOST

"Aaron didn't say anything at all from the time we left our house until we got to the Triphammer Mall, except 'Oh, wow!' when we were in the car wash and the suds and water were sloshing all over the car and making it look like we were in some kind of storm, which was great.

"He didn't say anything but that. 'Oh, wow!' It seems a very sad thing for his last words to us to be.

"Maybe not, though. Maybe not sad.

"I think that he's in the trees. I think that the eagle with the golden eyes got him.

"But I don't think it was an eagle at all. I've thought about this, and I don't think it was an eagle but something that wasn't a bird or an animal, and I think my brain changed it around to an eagle.

"When we pulled into our parking space, just before Aaron got lost, there were two cars beside us, one on one side and one on the other. I saw their license plates. The license plate numbers were . . ."

"But where can you look for him that you haven't already looked?" Lorraine asked.

Miles got his gray fall jacket from the closet near the front door, put it on, opened the door. "I have to look. I can't just stay here." He paused. "Are you coming with me?"

She shook her head. "I think it's possible that Aaron may come back, Miles. To this house."

He nodded. "Yes. I've thought of that."

"You go ahead. Do what you feel you have to. I'll stay here."

He nodded again, kissed her, told her he loved her, and left the house.

"I dreamed that my mother was talking to someone," C.J. told Irene Podkomiter, who had been pestering him for an hour about the dream that had made him wake up screaming.

Irene said, "The one who was . . . the one who died?"

C.J. nodded sullenly. "I dreamed that she was talking to someone," he repeated.

"To who?" asked Irene.

"To a woman."

"And that made you wake up screaming?"

"No."

"Then what?"

"Huh?"

"What made you wake up screaming?"

C.J. looked upset. He said, "I don't remember. I don't remember."

Carl Podkomiter, who had left to use the upstairs bathroom, reappeared in the kitchen, sat at the head of the table, and scanned the remains of breakfast—one wrinkled, graying sausage, two dried-out pancakes, and a teaspoon of runny scrambled egg. "Stop pestering him, Irene," he said.

"I wanna hear about this, Carl," she scolded.

"Let him eat," he said.

"He did eat."

"Doesn't look like it." C.J.'s plate of pancakes, sausage and eggs was all but untouched.

"Well, it's not like we haven't given him every opportunity," she said.

"I don't wanna eat," C.J. said. "And I don't wanna talk anymore, either."

"Dear," Irene said, "you've got to do one or the other."

"Why?"

"Because I said so."

"You're not my mother."

"That's true. But I do have responsibility for you."

"Leave him alone, Irene." Carl's voice held a weary resignation, as if he knew that his protests would be ignored. "Ask him if he's not going to eat his food if I could have it."

"He can have it," C.J. said.

"What a waste," Irene said, and handed her husband C.J.'s plate of food.

"It won't go to waste," he said. "I'll be eatin' it."

C.J. said, "Can I go back up to my room, now?"

Irene thought a moment, then said, "Yes, dear. But we'll be going out in an hour."

Triphammer Mall was closed until 12 noon. Sunday hours—12:00 to 7:30.

Miles peered into the mall, face pressed against the glass entrance doors, and scowled. "Goddammit!"

He thought it was possible that Aaron was hiding somewhere in the mall. The place was certainly big enough. One hundred stores, two levels, all kinds of places for a bright and rambunctious six-year-old to hide. It wasn't such a farfetched idea. It had only been sixteen days since Aaron's disappearance. Was it possible that the boy had found a comfortable, warm place to hide during the day, that he came out at night for food and entertainment, then returned to his hiding place? Hadn't he—Miles—read recently about a couple of boys who had actually spent *weeks* in the false ceiling of a large supermarket? Didn't they do just what he had supposed Aaron could be doing—coming out at night to eat, then going back up to their hiding place during the day?

But the stores here—at Triphammer Mall—were locked at night.

And the whole place was patrolled by security people with dogs.

Miles straightened from the glass entrance doors. He sighed. There was a quiver in the sigh—he was close to tears.

Aaron hiding out somewhere in the mall? It was a stupid and desperate idea.

He turned around and faced the midmorning November sun, which was very bright in a cloudless, light blue sky. "Aaron!" he screamed. "Aaron, where are you?"

A gull swooped over and screeched at him. He looked; it was very close. Why did gulls like parking lots? There were a couple dozen gulls nearby. Some walked about, heads bobbing comically with each step, some chased other gulls, necks straightened, wings beating furiously.

Miles yelled again, "Aaron? Answer me, Aaron. It's time to come home now."

But he got no answer.

He saw that the parking lot was beginning to fill with cars.

These words came to him: *I'm forgetting something. I'm not remembering something.*

After a while, he heard the mall doors behind him being unlocked.

Twelve noon.

He went inside.

NINE

Jessica French wrote, "I feel that C.J. Gale is repressing something. I feel that he's not telling me everything that happened on the day his brother disappeared. I have no concrete reason for feeling this way. I cannot say that he has been evasive, either in what he has written or said, verbally or in his demeanor. He is a very open child and I believe that he would find it quite difficult to knowingly lie. That, perhaps, goes to the heart of my intuition that he is not sharing with me all that his memory holds about his brother's disappearance. I believe it is possible that something traumatic happened to him on the day in question and that he has repressed it. I realize that this does not constitute a revelation, as the possibility of something traumatic happening (i.e., that his father, Dr. Miles Gale, was responsible for Aaron's disappearance) is precisely the reason C.J. is being held in a foster home until this whole bizarre and tragic situation is resolved."

Nine hours later, at just before three on Monday morning, seventeen days after Aaron's disappearance, Lorraine Rabkin woke because Miles was mumbling in his sleep.

She had awakened, as well, because of the wind.

It was fierce and loud. It didn't ebb and flow. It drove at

the house and made the windowpanes whine on one extended high note.

She thought that surely it would wake Miles.

"Miles?" she said.

He mumbled something she could not understand.

"Miles?"

"Ohh!" Miles said beside her in the bed. "Ohh!" as if he were seeing something very strange in his sleep.

"Miles?" she said.

"Ohh!" he said again, louder now. The word was closing in on panic and awe together, as if he were seeing a tidal wave that was building on the horizon and overtaking the sky above him.

"Miles, wake up!" She shook him.

In a voice that was high and fearful, as if his panic and awe and fear were pinching his vocal cords, he shouted, "My God! Aaron! My God!"

And the wind shrieked in the darkness around her.

It was in the room. It was a huge, shrieking, invisible creature and it was filling up the air in the room, stealing the air from her.

"Miles, wake up!" she screamed.

"Aaron!" he screamed.

She shook him violently.

Around them in the darkness the wind drew the oxygen off and she gasped for breath.

"Wake . . . up . . . Miles, wake . . . up!" she stammered.

"Marie!" he screamed.

She lunged for the bedside lamp on Miles's side of the bed, knocked it over, heard it crash distantly to the floor, a dull thud beneath the cacophony of the wind.

Miles sat up suddenly.

His chin connected with the side of Lorraine's head, and she screamed in pain.

Miles screamed, "Marie!"

The wind stopped all at once, as if it were the last clap of thunder in a storm.

"Dammit!" Lorraine whispered, and rubbed her head in the quiet darkness.

"Marie!" Miles breathed.

"You hurt me, Miles."

"Lorraine?" he said.

"You hit me in the head with your chin." She was sitting up on her side of the bed now.

"I was dreaming," he said. "I was dreaming about Marie." He paused. "It's so dark!" he whispered.

"I broke the lamp," Lorraine told him.

"The lamp?"

"Yes. I broke it. I was trying to turn it on."

Silence.

"Miles?"

"I was dreaming about Marie," he said again. "I was dreaming that Marie took Aaron. Lorraine, I dreamt that I *saw* her take Aaron. Two weeks ago. She was . . . there, and she took him."

"There?"

"When I saw the trees." A pause. "Oh, God!"

"Miles, please . . ." She got out of bed. "I'm turning on the damn light. It's too dark in here."

"My God, my God!"

"Miles—" She came around to his side of the bed in the darkness, sat down on the bed, hugged him. "What's wrong?"

"I saw her. I remember now—I saw her, and she took Aaron. She was there, and she took him."

"No, Miles, that's not possible."

But it was possible, and she knew it.

Because she was convinced that Marie had been her friend long before Marie had been Miles's wife.

TEN

It was Monday afternoon and Detective Vinikoff was at
Modern Kids, a toy store in Triphammer Mall. He was
looking at a sign above a display of wooden toys; the
sign read PLEASE DON'T PLAY WITH TOYS! He smiled. It was
a ludicrous suggestion, he thought. Toys were meant to be
played with, after all.

The store's proprietor, a tall, balding man of sixty who
smiled often, and nervously, came over and asked if he
could help Vinikoff.

The detective produced his badge, and asked, "Were you
here last Monday? About this time."

"I'm here every day, sir," the proprietor answered.
"From nine in the morning until closing, which varies."

"Do you remember the commotion out there?" He gestured to indicate the mall area.

"You mean the man who lost his little boy? Oh, yes."

"Do you remember anything specific?"

"Specific?"

"Yes. Do you remember seeing the man himself calling
for his son?"

"No." He shook his head. "No, I can't say that I remember that. But it was a while ago, and there are many, many

things that go on in that mall, and it is not to say that the man was *not* calling to his son."

Vinikoff nodded. "Thanks," he said, then tapped the sign above the wooden toys. "You need a 'the' here."

" 'The'?"

Vinikoff nodded again. "Uh-huh. After the word 'with.' It should say, 'Please don't play with *the* toys.' "

The proprietor looked confusedly at the sign, then looked confusedly at Vinikoff. "Is that all?"

"Uh-huh. Just 'the.' Then it would make sense. As it is—"

"I meant," the proprietor interrupted, "do you have any other questions?"

Vinikoff frowned. "Not at the moment." He nodded to indicate the wooden toys. "I didn't realize you could buy toys like this anymore."

"You mean the wooden toys?"

"Uh-huh. So many damned *plastic* toys everywhere you look. It's nice to know that you can still find real wooden toys. My sister's kids would love 'em."

"These are antiques, sir. They're not for sale."

"Oh," Vinikoff said, crestfallen. "Sure." He looked nostalgically at the wooden toys for a moment—there were tractors, cars, a wooden tugboat, a small train set—then left the store.

Jessica French said to C.J. Gale, who was seated in front of Jessica's desk, "How are you getting along at the Podkomiters'? They're nice people, aren't they?"

C.J. said nothing.

"Do you have a problem with the Podkomiters, C.J.?"

He shook his head reluctantly.

"If you don't like it there, we can look into finding other accommo—"

"When are you going to let me go back and live with my dad?" C.J. interrupted.

"I'm afraid that's a hard question to answer, C.J. We have a very complex situation that we're trying to unravel. I'm sure you can appreciate that."

"I don't sleep too good at that house."

"At the Podkomiters'?"

C.J. nodded sullenly. Jessica thought the boy looked even paler than the last time they'd talked, three days earlier. "I woke up last night and I was screaming."

"From a bad dream, you mean?"

C.J. nodded, eyes lowered, hands folded tightly in his lap, so his knuckles were red. "A bad dream. Yeah."

"Do you remember it?"

He nodded once, meaningfully.

"You remember the dream, C.J.?"

"Yes."

"Do you want to share it with me?"

He shook his head earnestly, eyes still lowered. "No. If I tell it to you, it'll come back again tonight and I'll wake up screaming again."

Jessica thought about this. She wanted to tell C.J. that sharing the dream might exorcise it, then it would be gone forever. But if the boy believed that sharing the dream would cause it to recur, then perhaps it would, simply because he believed it would.

Jessica said, "Was it about your brother? Was it about Aaron?"

C.J. looked shocked. "I *said* that I didn't want to talk about it."

Jessica sighed. Wasn't this behavior simply further proof

of the intuition she had about Aaron's disappearance, that C.J. was repressing something traumatic? She decided to press on. "Then it *was* about Aaron?"

"I told you, I *don't* want to talk about it," C.J. snapped, and threw himself to his feet suddenly, thrust his hands into the pockets of his harshly creased black pants, and lowered his head.

"C.J. What's wrong?"

He shook his head fiercely, eyes still lowered, then looked up for a moment. There was fear in his gray eyes. And regret. He lowered his head again and whispered, "I lied."

"I'm sorry, C.J. I didn't hear you. Did you say that you lied?"

He nodded. His head was still lowered, hands still thrust into the pockets of his pants.

He raised his head. His eyes were rimmed with red; he was on the verge of tears. "I lied, Dr. French. I'm sorry. I lied!"

"About what, C.J.?"

He shook his head. "About Aaron and about how he got lost. I lied."

Jessica nodded to indicate the black metal chair just behind him. "Sit down, C.J." She tried to sound reassuring. "We'll talk about it, okay?"

C.J. plopped into the chair. He began to shiver, and put his long arms around himself, as if he were cold.

Jessica stood, came around the desk, went to him, hugged him. "It's all right, C.J. Everything's all right," she said.

C.J., his head pressed into Jessica's chest, whimpered, "Everything's not all right. Aaron's never coming back. Never!"

Six Years Earlier

Miles says into his tape recorder, "The skeletons are heavy-boned, with strong muscular attachment, and the heads are broad, round, and of medium height in the vault. Cranial capacity is good."

Five-year-old C.J., listening nearby, asks, "What are malars?"

Miles answers, "Cheekbones, sport," points at his cheekbones, and goes on talking into his tape recorder. "All of the skeletons, and skulls, except for the individual whose skull was located at grid three, were heavily pressure-fractured from the weight of the earth on them.

"It was obvious that the female skull found at grid three was not of the same group. The skull is of exceptional cranial capacity, certainly higher than the rest of the group, and is narrow, oval, and very high in the vault, with almost no eyebrow or temporal ridges. The cheekbones are similar to the Frontenac island people, however, although the nose is narrow, and long, much more Caucasian than the rest of the group.

"It can only be assumed that this individual was a visitor, though we have found no other Archaic evidence of people similar to her."

ELEVEN

Miles Gale pointed at a big open area above a bank of restaurants at the center of Triphammer Mall—the restaurants had been built around a large indoor pavilion; there were people eating in this pavilion, and people eating around it, at small, rectangular tables made of white plastic. "What's up there?" Miles asked. "I've noticed that before. It looks like it's an open space."

He was talking to the mall's maintenance supervisor, Mr. Carey—tall, lanky, clean-shaven. Carey nodded. "Uh-huh, that's the employee dining room. People who work at the mall buy their food down here and they take it up there." He pointed at a door between a restaurant called Panda Chinese and one called Sicilian Delights. (The signs for the restaurants all had been done in bright neon; PANDA CHINESE was red, SICILIAN DELIGHTS green on a white background; other colorful signs, all of them in neon, reflected the particular restaurant's menu, or theme. The whole look was modernist art deco, unified and off-putting all together, but, singly, oddly appealing.) The door Mr. Carey was pointing at was unlabeled and closed. "The dining room's not being used now because they're working on it, you know," he went on. "But that's the entrance."

"Are there separate rooms up there?" Miles asked. "Or is it one big open room?"

"Mostly one big open room. There are a couple of storerooms." He tilted his head, clearly suspicious. "Why do you want to know?"

Miles shook his head. "No reason. I'm interested in architecture. I was just wondering."

Carey gave him an odd look, said, "Sure. Good talking with you," and started to move off when Miles called after him, "One more question, if you don't mind."

Carey looked back. He wasn't far off. "Shoot," he said.

Miles asked, "You've probably been to every nook and cranny in this mall; would you say there are a lot of . . . hiding places? I mean, if a person, a kid, wanted to hide in here, could he do it without getting caught?"

Carey shrugged. "Sure. I guess. I never thought about it." He shrugged again. "Probably if you worked hard enough at it, you could hide in here. Course, the stores get locked up at night—"

"Yes, I know."

"And the whole place is patrolled—"

"I'm aware of that."

"But I guess if you wanted to hide in here—" He nodded at the pavilion. Large enough to hold half a hundred people, it was covered by a gazebo-style roof; its underside was skirted by a stylized white trellis. "If you wanted to, I guess you could hide under there. Or you could put yourself in one of the storerooms above." He nodded to indicate the open area. "And wait until the mall closed." He shrugged. "But why would anyone want to do that? What would it gain them?"

Miles said nothing.

*　*　*

Jessica French held C.J.'s chin in her hand and looked very earnestly and very sympathetically into his gray eyes. "What you're telling me, C.J., is just not possible. Certainly you're aware of that."

"It happened," he said simply, voice hoarse from emotion.

Jessica shook her head. "No. You *believe* that it happened. And while, certainly, that's a very concrete yardstick for what is real and what isn't, in this case what *you* believe happened can have no bearing whatever on what *could* have happened. Do you follow me?" She felt miserable. Of course the boy wasn't following her. "Something inside you, in your head"—she let go of his chin; he let his head lower slightly, though he still kept his eyes on hers—"made this whole thing up to . . . hide from you, from your conscious mind, what *really* happened."

He shook his head. "No. What I told you happened *really* happened. I'm not lying."

"You misunderstand me, C.J. I'm not accusing you of lying. I know that you wouldn't lie. I'm telling you that what actually happened two weeks ago, when Aaron disappeared, was so . . . traumatic . . ." She paused, then continued. "Do you know what that means?"

"Yes."

"Good."

"And I know what you're trying to say, too. You're trying to say that I saw my dad do something terrible to Aaron and it was so traumatic I . . . that something inside me, in my subconscious, made up all the stuff I told you so I wouldn't remember it. But that's not *true,* Dr. French. What I *told* you is true."

Jessica sighed, straightened, pushed her hands down her thighs to smooth out her skirt. "What you're going to have to face, C.J., if we're ever going to find Aaron, is the fact that the story you told me, as fanciful as it is, *couldn't* be true. Just like it couldn't be true that the moon is made of green cheese, or that the oceans are going to boil away—"

"They will someday."

"Don't interrupt me, C.J. This is a very, very serious matter. You know what I'm telling you. And what I want you to do is to go back to the Podkomiters' tonight, and when you come to see me again tomorrow, I want you to be able to talk about what *really* happened. Or at least make a stab at it. Okay?"

He looked pleadingly up at her, but said nothing.

TWELVE

H e should have kept trying to call Lorraine's office at the university, Miles thought. She'd be worried. She'd wonder where he was. Maybe he could find a phone when he got out of here. Lorraine would be waiting for him at his house; he'd call her there and tell her what he was doing.

He listened but heard nothing from outside the door. Perhaps he could at last do what he had come here to do.

He hadn't dared to move for hours, afraid that someone might hear him, and consequently, his legs were asleep. He massaged them. If he tried to stand now, he'd fall flat on his face. His neck hurt, too. This small space wasn't meant for hiding.

What time was it? Ten? Eleven? Later than that? He tried to read his watch in the darkness, but its luminous dial was unreadable; light hadn't hit it for a long time. He held the dial very close to his eyes. Nothing. He put the watch to his ear. *Tick, tick*. What a gracious invention—an electronic watch that ticked. The ticking of a watch was reassuring, somehow. It was natural. Watches that merely hummed weren't natural or reassuring.

He stiffened. Had he heard someone talking beyond the door? He strained to hear. He heard what sounded like a distant wind. That was reasonable. He was near the roof of the mall, and if there was a wind above, it was logical to assume that he'd hear it. What had the weather forecast been? Wind? Rain?

Again he heard what could have been voices. He stopped breathing and listened intently in the total darkness. Again he heard what sounded like a wind.

Jessica French wrote, "C.J. is a very imaginative child. I would not have expected it, especially considering his photographic memory. The additional gift of a fertile imagination would seem unlikely under the burden of so much information to sift through and make sense of. But I have underestimated him severely. He is a very bright and very imaginative boy, but he is very disturbed, too, and I think that the events of the past weeks have contributed greatly to that.

"The story he told me today, about the disappearance of his brother Aaron, was without precedent in my experience, even from the very imaginative. It seems likely that it was designed, by his subconscious, to cushion him from what appears to be the increasingly strong possibility that Aaron was the victim of foul play, that, indeed, as C.J. says, Aaron is 'never coming back.' Concocting the story he told me is at least a way of keeping his brother amongst the living, if unreachable. This is an understandable response to tragedy, but it is nonetheless highly regrettable and indicates that C.J. may descend even further into the welcoming embrace of fantasy before he admits the truth about his brother's disappearance."

Irene Podkomiter was peeking in on C.J. She had peeked in on him several times each night during his stay here. She had poked her head in through the doorway, waited a second, whispered, "Asleep, dear?" and, getting no answer, even though, unknown to her, C.J. was awake, withdrew her head and closed the door.

C.J. watched her now in the darkness, as he had done each night here, and saw the black oval of her face, the fringe of blondish hair sifting the light.

"Asleep, dear?"

C.J. didn't answer.

She withdrew her head, closed the door, and plunged the little room into darkness.

"You know what *I* think," he heard her say distantly. *"I* think he's awake. I think he's in there looking at me. And *that's* spooky! One of these times I'm going to turn on—" He heard a door slam and her voice was gone.

He recalled again, as if in fast review, the exact words he had said to Dr. French earlier that day, about Aaron's disappearance.

Then he whispered, "I'm crazy." He smiled ruefully. "I'm crazy as a bat."

Miles remembered that there was a mop in a blue plastic bucket beside him, to his right, and a box of Spic 'n' Span to his left. He could feel the soft, smooth plastic bucket against his bare elbow.

He wondered, suddenly, why he wasn't seeing the narrow strip of dull yellow light beneath the door anymore. Had the lights in the mall been turned off? It seemed unlikely. How would the security people and their dogs see what they were doing?

Perhaps something was blocking the light. Perhaps someone had put something in front of the door and it was blocking the light.

He didn't think so. There was absolutely *no* light here. It was as if he'd gone blind.

And there, again, was the sound of wind. Less distant. Closer above him. He thought he could hear the acoustic ceiling tiles rattling sympathetically.

Marie, he thought.

Golden eyes.

Marie had golden eyes.

Why was it so incredibly dark in here? Beyond the closed door there was light that had been muted only a little for the hours that the mall remained closed. There were huge rectangular fluorescents hanging twenty feet above the mall's bottom level, and neon signs in garish colors, and store interior lights that cast soft shadows; enough light to read by. A cloudy-day sort of light. Dusk light.

But there was no light here. Nothing filtered through under the closed door.

He couldn't see his watch, and he couldn't hear it because of the wind.

Marie, he thought. *Golden eyes.*

The wind rattled the acoustic ceiling tiles.

He massaged his legs furiously. They were asleep, they tingled.

No light. He couldn't see himself massaging his legs. He couldn't hear his own breathing, although he had heard it before.

No light. The dull hiss of wind rattling the acoustic ceiling tiles.

What's going on here? he asked himself.

He heard more than wind, more than acoustic ceiling tiles rattling.

He heard the rushing noise of leaves being pushed by wind. Leaves turning over, exposing their pale undersides.

In the dark.
He massaged his legs.
He did not move.
He couldn't move.

Jessica French wrote, "There is much wish fulfillment in
the story C.J. tells. Reconstructing and reordering the present; recalling the past for the purposes of that reconstruc-
tion. Putting himself, in effect, in a time before the time of
the traumatic events he was forced to witness. It could even
be said that by recalling the past, and making it the present,
he is subconsciously able to cancel the existence of those
people who have apparently brought him so much sor-
row—Marie, who is his missing stepmother, and Miles
Gale, his father.

"As preliminary as these ideas are, I would have to say
that they revolve around one irrefutable fact: that the disappearance of Aaron Gale was not as Miles Gale or, for
complex reasons already touched upon, C.J. Gale, have
described it."

She signed the report, and dated it.

Marie's portrait still stood on the mantel at Miles's
house. Pictures of Miles's first wife, Joanna, and of C.J.,
and Aaron—singly and together—stood nearby. A pair of
small brass wall lamps hung above the mantel and they
illuminated the photographs from above. The illumination
was not good. The photographs in their frames stood back
a little from the wall lamps and leaned backwards, as well,
so the light from the lamps made the top half of the photographs too bright, and the bottom half too dark. This effect
was reversed depending upon the viewpoint of the observer,
and his height. C.J. and Aaron, looking up at the photo-

graphs, invariably saw the reflection of the lamps themselves, and little, if anything, of the portraits. This pleased
C.J., who didn't like looking at pictures of Marie, or of
himself. Aaron wasn't bothered by it because he had a little
photograph album of his own and there were dozens of
pictures of his mother in it. He adored his mother. It had
been the major tragedy of his young life when she had
disappeared eighteen months earlier. He had withdrawn
into months of depression and noncommunication, and
only after more months of therapy had he begun to emerge
from his self-imposed isolation.

Lorraine, looking at the portrait of Marie from several
feet away, saw Marie's eyes, her high cheekbones, her high,
sloping forehead, and the crown of black hair that had hung
nearly to her waist. She could not see Marie's mouth
clearly. It was obscured by tricks of reflection and refrac-
tion.

"What have you done?" Lorraine whispered. The portrait grinned. The obscured mouth twisted at its right-hand
corner, and Lorraine thought, *This is only something I'm
imagining.*

She stepped forward. Marie's golden eyes, high forehead,
crown of dark hair, and prominent cheekbones all vanished
into darkness, and her mouth appeared. It was very full,
red, lovely.

Marie had been an exquisitely beautiful woman.

The mouth in the portrait wasn't grinning. It was parted
in a sensual smile. Lorraine saw a hint of teeth.

"How well did I know you, Marie?" she whispered.

She lingered on the portrait for a long moment. Then she
shrugged out of her coat, set it on the couch, called "Miles?
You asleep? Sorry I'm so late," and started up the stairs to
the bedroom.

Six Years Earlier

It is June seventeenth, two months before Joanna's murder, and Miles is taking C.J. to the dig at Frontenac Island. Joanna isn't feeling well and has asked Miles to take care of C.J. for the afternoon.

Father and son get to the island in a small aluminum motorboat owned by the university; Miles puts a life jacket on C.J. for the short trip—the island is only a stone's throw from shore—but does not wear one himself. "The water's only up to here on me, sport," he says, and holds his hand up to the middle of his chest.

When they're halfway to the island, C.J. sees that there are other people on the island—a short, thin man who wears a green floppy hat on his gray head, and a tall woman with long, red hair; she walks a little bit ahead of the man.

"Jack, Helen," Miles calls over the sputter of the little outboard motor. "Did you bring the beer and hot dogs?"

"What?" Jack hollers.

Miles shakes his head and hollers back, "Never mind. Bad joke."

The Gales reach the shore a minute later and climb out of the aluminum boat onto a short, makeshift wooden dock. Helen picks C.J. up and holds him on her arm. "Little doll," she coos, while Jack rubs C.J.'s head and says, "This is a good training ground for a budding archaeologist, Miles."

"Jo wasn't feeling well," Miles explains. "She asked if I could bring him with me. Besides, he wants to see what a dig is all about."

"Sure," Jack says, and smilingly rubs C.J.'s head again.

Helen puts C.J. on the ground, which is soft and almost

black. It's like walking on ashes. "Don't wander off, little guy," she says.

Miles takes hold of C.J.'s hand and says, "I guess we'll have to keep a close eye on you, won't we, sport? Don't want this damned island sucking you up." He looks at Jack. "Anything new here?"

"Not a whole hell of a lot, Miles. We've begun work on grid twenty-three." He points toward the back of the island. "But we haven't found much of interest. Some evidence of the use of ochre, which I found unusual. And we've located a woman and her infant. That's not in grid twenty-three. It's in grid fourteen."

Miles asks, "Same anomaly we've seen before?"

Jack nods. "Yes. Damned odd, too."

Helen says, "As you know, Miles—and this is not the first time you've heard this, I'm sure—I am of the opinion that a virus is responsible for what we're seeing here, and I don't think it would be overly cautious to put this island under quarantine."

Miles says, "This site is over six thousand years old, Helen."

"Yes, and the wheat found at Cheops was four thousand years old. But it still grew."

"I take your point," Miles says. "However, we've had specialists examine the site, and the remains, and they've concluded, as you know, Helen—"

She interrupts, "Yes, I know what their conclusions are, Miles. I simply think it would be smart to err on the side of caution."

"It would be smart not to err at all, Helen," Miles says. "I'm convinced that there's no virus present. Hell, would I bring *him* here"—he nods at C.J.—"if I believed otherwise?"

<u>THIRTEEN</u>

Miles felt compelled to stand. The situation demanded it. So he stood, clumsily, knocking over the bucket and mop and banging his head on a shelf above. The shelf wasn't anchored to the wall brackets so it clattered to the floor. He heard none of the noise these events created. He was only distantly aware of them. He was aware of the darkness and of the sound of leaves being turned over and over in a staccato fashion, like gunfire, by the awful wind above.

He reached for the doorknob, fingers trembling, but couldn't easily gauge where it was in the darkness, couldn't remember how deep this storage space was. His outstretched fingers hit the door and he recoiled. The metal door was very cold, much colder than it should have been.

He shook his head, reached again, found the doorknob, grasped it, turned it. Froze.

Things don't happen like this, he thought frantically. His was a universe of art deco neon, brand names, fluorescent lights, computers, modern fashion.

That was the universe which existed beyond the closed door.

He pulled on the knob.

The door wouldn't open.

He caught his breath. Of course. The door opened outward. More storage space that way. A reasonable design in a reasonable universe.

He pushed on the knob.

He let it go.

The door swung open.

Marie was there, grinning, framed by the darkness.

And she peered in at him with golden eyes.

FOURTEEN

Darling Miles," she said. Her voice was the clear, high voice of wind. Behind her, the trees—maple, oak, pine, tulip—swayed right and left as easily as flowers. As they swayed they alternately obscured, revealed, obscured a field of bright stars in a dense black sky.

Miles stared in awe at her.

"I have him," she screeched. "I have my son forever!" She grabbed the doorknob, said again, "Forever!" And threw the door shut.

The wind stilled.

Light showed beneath the door.

And an anxious voice from below called, "What was that?"

"Jesus, someone's up there," called another voice.

Miles sat down slowly on the overturned bucket and mop, and on the shelf that had fallen from above.

He waited.

Soon, the closet door opened. A dog snarled at him, and a voice from behind the snarling dog commanded, "Get up outa there!"

WHAT REALLY HAPPENED THE DAY
AARON GOT LOST

"We went to the car wash in Dad's new car. We got the car washed there and a man named Dave took our money. He smiled. It was a big smile and I thought that he meant it. His eyes were brown.

"We went to Triphammer Mall after that, and as we turned into the parking lot I saw the trees. Lots of trees!

"It was a forest. Not just a few trees, not just one or two trees, but a whole forest.

"So I said to Aaron, who was reading *Masters of the Universe,* 'Aaron, oh . . .' And I didn't say anything more because then the forest was gone and the mall was back and I was looking at a little black dog that was running loose, and I turned my head again and I said to Aaron, 'Look at that dog. He might get hit,' because I had forgotten about seeing the forest. I saw it for a couple seconds, then I didn't see it, then I forgot about it. And I *never* forget. But I forgot that.

"And then Dad was pulling the car into the parking area and we were all looking for a parking space, and that is when I saw Marie. She was watching us. She wasn't far away, she was standing in front of a store that's called J.C. Penney's, and she was wearing a long blue dress and standing very still, staring at us.

"I said to Dad, 'Look at that woman. She looks like Marie.' But he didn't hear me because he was busy looking for a parking space. He had the radio up loud. It was playing a song called *Rainy Day Women,* by Bob Dylan.

"The song stopped all of a sudden when Dad pulled the car into a parking space.

"He didn't turn off the radio and he didn't turn off the car engine. The radio just stopped playing all of a sudden.

"And I looked at it because I thought there was something wrong with it, I thought that maybe it had broken, and I was going to say to Dad that it was crummy if the radio in his new car broke. And when I looked up at Dad to say this I saw green all around the car. Out the front windows and the side windows and the back windows. Green. And trees all around us. No mall. Just green trees, and bits of blue sky.

"And Marie was standing right next to the car, right next to the back door, next to where Aaron was sitting, and he was still reading his *Masters of the Universe* comic book and didn't see what I was seeing, or Dad, who was seeing it too, I could tell, because when I looked at him I saw that his eyes were very wide and his mouth was open, and there was noise, too. Wind blowing real hard through the trees. Wind. I could hear it in the trees. Wind in the trees.

"And then Marie opened Aaron's door and reached in and grabbed him by the arm and took him out of the car, and I think he said 'Mommy?' I wasn't sure. He said it very low, and I couldn't hear much because of the wind, and I looked at Dad and said to him, 'Aaron's gone.' "

In the storage space on the second level of the Triphammer Mall, Miles heard, "Put your hands behind your back, please."

He didn't respond.

"Put your *hands* behind your *back!*"

He did it. Distantly, he felt handcuffs being put on his wrists, tightened, locked.

"Did you read him his rights?"

"Yes."

"What's your name, sir?"

Miles said nothing. He couldn't remember his name.

"Could you tell me your name?"

"Miles," he heard himself whisper.

"Miles what?"

Nothing. He couldn't remember his surname.

"Look in his wallet."

"I'll get it."

Miles heard himself whisper "Gale," and felt his hands being moved to one side, his wallet being taken from his back pocket.

"Gale," he heard himself repeat. "Gale." It seemed oddly unfamiliar, as if it were the name of someone he'd known in grade school and hadn't seen since.

"Gale, Miles," he heard. "Age thirty-eight, address—" The voice went on to give Miles's address. And that, too, as Miles listened, seemed oddly unfamiliar. A stranger's address.

"What are you doing here, Mr. Gale?"

"Dr. Gale," one of the voices corrected.

"Doctor?"

"Sure. It's right here. Doctor Gale. He's connected with the university, apparently."

University? Miles wondered. He couldn't remember.

"What are you doing in the mall, Dr. Gale? Did you know that it was closed?"

Miles felt himself shaking his head. He heard himself whisper, "Marie. She's here."

"Who?" a voice asked.

Miles didn't answer. Who was Marie? Why had he said her name?

"Did somebody else come in here with you, Dr. Gale?"

"Yes," he said. The name seemed more familiar now. "Marie. She's here."

"Marie?"

"Did he say 'Marie'?"

"Who is this 'Marie,' Dr. Gale?"

"My wife," he said, and thought it could have been a question. Had he been married to someone named Marie? He couldn't remember. At last, he nodded a little. "She was . . . my wife."

"And she's here, too?"

"No."

"He's lying."

"Where is Marie, Dr. Gale?"

"Not here. She's not here."

"He's lying."

"She's gone," Miles said.

"Gone? Could you explain that, Dr. Gale?"

"No."

"Was she here with you?"

"Yes."

"Is she still here?"

"I don't know."

"Jesus, this is getting nowhere."

"I don't remember," Miles said.

FIFTEEN

The detective, his name was McDaniels, asked, "You were in the mall looking for your son?"

Miles nodded dully. He was seated next to the detective's desk in a straight-backed, blue metal chair, and his gaze was on the squad room's far wall, which was not far away. The wall had a duty roster and a calendar on it. Because it was December first, the calendar showed a Christmas scene. Miles was focusing on the Christmas scene—in the foreground there was a snow-covered bridge; trees and farmhouse lay beyond. A horse-drawn sleigh, bulging with gaily wrapped presents, was halfway across the bridge, and a happy nineteenth-century family crowded the gaily wrapped presents. It was a very stylized scene that tried hard to simulate a Currier & Ives print, but it was too colorful, too angular, too clearly a rendering of a late nineteenth-century event done by an artist whose intellect and spirit were trapped in the 1990s.

Detective McDaniels went on, "I've got your file, Dr. Gale." A pause. "Could you look at me when I'm talking to you, please."

Miles looked at him.

McDaniels held up a thick manila folder. "I found this very interesting. Very informative."

"Did you?" Miles said, without interest.

"Yes, I did." He set the file folder on his desk.

Miles looked at the calendar again. He saw the sleigh move a little, saw the mouths of the happy family open in gaiety and good feeling, heard the rush of the sleigh's runners over the soft snow.

"Please look at me, Dr. Gale."

Miles looked at McDaniels. "Am I being charged with trespassing?" Miles asked.

"In all likelihood, yes."

"Oh."

"No formal complaint has yet been made by the mall's owners, but I expect it momentarily."

Miles said nothing. He turned his gaze once more to the calendar. The sleigh was stationary, the people frozen in time (whatever time it was; 1990, 1890), the whole scene static. He frowned.

"You're free to call your lawyer, Dr. Gale," McDaniels said.

Miles said nothing.

McDaniels opened the file on his desk. He said, "You're an archaeologist?"

Miles ignored him.

"That's what the 'Dr.' means?"

Miles continued to ignore him. He watched the happy family come back to life, watched the sleigh move an inch, a foot, watched it clear the bridge and leave the farmhouse far behind, watched a new snowfall come and add a couple of inches to the foot of soft snow that was already on the ground, watched the sky clear, watched noisily squawking geese fly over.

"I'm talking to you."

The happy family appeared once more on the bridge. They crowded the gaily wrapped presents. The presents crowded them. They were caught motionless on the bridge forever.

Six Years Earlier

Marie says, "You give me life."

"That's a strange remark," Miles says.

"Only a gesture of thanks." Marie is hugging him. They're standing naked in the bedroom. The door's open, and C.J. is watching them from the darkness of the hallway.

"Thanks?" Miles says to Marie. "For what?"

"For giving me life."

Miles smiles at her. "You give *me* life."

Marie sees C.J. looking at them from the hallway. She gives him an angry look.

"There's no need to get so upset with him," Miles says.

"He was spying on me, Miles. I won't have it!"

"Existence," Miles began, and leaned over in his blue metal chair so his elbows were on Detective McDaniels's desk and his hands were clasped tightly; his green eyes blazed with meaning as he continued, "is not as dependable or as predictable as you have always believed."

"I'm sure you're right," McDaniels said dryly.

Miles looked at him for a moment. The fire left his eyes; he sat back in his chair and tried to focus again on the Christmas calendar. He couldn't. The picture had lost its appeal and its magic. He had consumed it, had used up the split second in time that it represented, had made as much of it as could be made of it.

Perhaps it would come alive again of its own accord, without his coaxing. But probably not.

The universe was 99.99% predictable, after all. The calendar would remain forever only a piece of thick paper covered by printer's ink.

Three Years Earlier

C.J. is telling his little brother Aaron a joke: "This little boy said to his father, 'Daddy, what's a penis?' And the father said—"

"Penis?" Aaron interrupts.

"Just listen, okay."

"Okay."

"Good," C.J. says, and continues, "And the father said, 'I'll show you.' And he took off his pants and pointed at his penis and said, 'This is a penis.' "

"Penis?" Aaron says again.

"Just *listen*," C.J. commands.

Aaron falls silent.

Marie comes into the room, looks at Aaron, then sternly at C.J. and demands, "What are you doing with my son?"

C.J. shakes his head. "I'm not doing anything. I'm sorry."

"If you're not doing anything, then why are you sorry?" Marie says.

"I don't know."

"Ha," she says. "There's a *hell* of a lot you *don't know,* boy!" And she reaches out her hand to Aaron and says, "Come with me."

"But C.J. is telling me a joke," Aaron says.

"No," Marie says. "No jokes."

And he gets up and leaves the room with her.

"Dammit, where *are* you, Miles?" Lorraine whispered to herself. "Where *are* you?"

She sensed that he was in trouble. It was not an overwhelming intuition, just a niggling sense of unease, as if she were coming down with a flu and it was in its earliest stages.

She poured herself another cup of coffee from the percolator, thought that she probably shouldn't be having so much coffee—she glanced behind her at the kitchen clock above the sink—at three in the morning, but it was probable that this waiting would go on until dawn, and there was no way she was going to be able to sleep, anyway. She sipped the coffee, burned the tip of her tongue, set the mug down hard on the counter.

"Dammit!" she whispered, and touched the tip of her tongue with her thumb and forefinger, as if there were some injury there that she could actually feel. "Dammit!" she whispered again. She had known the coffee was hot.

Sliding glass doors led to the patio. She was facing them, her gaze on the area of the white counter and the coffee mug. She could see the doors, and the darkness beyond, in the top half of her field of view.

Something large came and went in the darkness beyond the sliding glass doors. She looked up, startled, but saw nothing.

She stared at the darkness as she caressed the warm and soothing mug of coffee with her hand.

"Is someone out there?" she called.

She hesitated, went around the counter, with her coffee mug in hand, to the sliding glass doors. When she looked out she saw nothing at all, as if someone had taped black crepe paper on the window and it was blocking her view of the other houses, the spotlights, the creamy horizon, where the city should have been. She put her face to the glass and her left hand up to block the glare from the lights in the kitchen.

She saw huge, hulking dark shapes beyond the window.

She straightened. "Uh—" she said.

She looked again. *Trees?* she realized.

She reached, hesitated, opened the sliding glass doors, and stepped out into the night.

SIXTEEN

Three Years Earlier

Aaron comes into C.J.'s bedroom and says to C.J., "Can you finish telling me that joke about the penis?"

"Is your mother around?" C.J. asks.

Aaron shakes his head. "No, she's not around. She's at the store."

"Okay, then," C.J. says. "I'll finish telling you the joke."

Aaron smiles and shuts the door.

C.J. says, "So the father pulled down his pants and said to the little boy, 'See, now this is a penis.' And then he didn't say anything for a moment. Then he said, 'In fact, it's a perfect penis.' "

"Perfect penis," Aaron giggles, and adds, "What's a penis, C.J.?"

"Just listen, okay," C.J. admonishes.

"Is it a wee-wee?" Aaron asks.

"Yeah, it's a wee-wee. Now let me finish telling the joke, okay."

"Okay."

"Good." C.J. pauses and continues, "Then, the next day, the little boy went to school and his friends said to him,

'What's a penis?' And the little boy pulled down his pants
and pointed at himself and said, 'This is a penis.' Then he
said, 'And if it was two inches shorter, it would be a perfect
penis.' " C.J. laughs, but Aaron frowns and asks, "Why
would it be perfect, C.J.?"

C.J. doesn't know, so he doesn't answer. He asks if
Aaron wants to play with Matchbox cars.

"Yes," Aaron answers, clapping his hands together. "I
would like to play with the Matchbox cars, now."

And C.J. drags the box of Matchbox cars out from under
the bed.

The owners of the Triphammer Mall, after being told
why Miles had hidden himself in one of their storage closets, did not press charges, and Miles was allowed to go
home after spending the night in a holding cell. He was very
tired. The bed in the cell had been lumpy and hard, and he
ached. He wanted to sleep, wanted to forget what he had
seen the night before, found himself actually manufacturing
other memories to take the place of reality: He saw himself
pushing the storage closet door open and seeing only the
snarling face of the dog; he saw himself pushing the door
open, seeing darkness, and hearing from below, "What
happened to the damned lights?" These images, these re-
placements for reality, were almost convincing.

But he felt disoriented, now. Out of place. He felt *dis-
placed,* as if he were trapped in a country whose language
was foreign to him.

"Lorraine?" he called. He closed his front door behind
him, opened the foyer closet door, and hung up his jacket.
He supposed that Lorraine was at work, that she had probably left a note.

He went into the kitchen and looked about. No note. Everything was in order.

He dialed Lorraine's office number, got her secretary, was told that Lorraine hadn't shown up for work yet. He hung up, went back to the living room. "Lorraine?" he called up the stairs.

Nothing.

WHAT HAPPENED THE DAY AARON GOT LOST

"And when Marie took Aaron she slammed the door shut and I turned to Dad and said, 'Aaron's gone.'

"But Dad didn't say anything. I think that he was too surprised by the trees all around.

" 'Aaron's gone,' I said again.

"Dad said, 'Where *are* we?' He whispered it. He was scared. I was scared, too. I don't think I was as scared as him. I don't know.

"I forgot everything. Why would that *happen?*

"I think that Dad forgot everything, too.

"Then the trees were gone and the mall was back. Dad sat staring straight ahead for a long time."

Miles checked the master bedroom. The bed was made; perhaps it had been slept in, perhaps not. Lorraine was a stickler for a neat bed.

He went to C.J.'s room and found it empty.

He went to Aaron's room; he found it empty, too.

He went to the guest bedroom. Lorraine was there, asleep, the blankets pulled up over her head, which was the way she often slept, especially here, in this house.

He nudged her. "Lorraine?" he said softly. She didn't stir. She was facing away from him. He nudged her again. "Lorraine, wake up."

One arm flew out from under the blankets and pushed at the air near his face. "Leave me alone!" she murmured testily.

"It's me, Miles," he said. "Wake up, okay?"

She pushed at the air again. "Go away!"

She was still asleep, he realized. He nudged her a third time, harder. "We've got to talk, Lorraine." It had always been difficult to wake her. Often, when he thought she was awake—after they had had an extended, and sometimes very animated, conversation, for instance—she would shake her head and say something that would tell him she had been asleep the whole time.

"Go away," she said again, and rolled over suddenly and faced him, though her head was still covered by the blanket. She grabbed his hand and squeezed it very hard.

"Are you awake?" he asked.

Her head under the brown blanket nodded.

"Is that a yes?"

There was no nod.

"Are you really awake?"

She let go of his hand. "I didn't know Marie," she said from under the blanket.

"I don't understand," Miles said.

She rolled to her back so her red hair appeared above the blanket. Then her forehead appeared as the blanket fell over her face.

She pulled the blanket down and gasped a little, as if it had been robbing her of air. Her eyes were closed. She kept them closed as she spoke. "Something happened to me last night, Miles," she whispered.

"Something happened to you?" Miles said. *"What* happened to you?"

She shook her head. "I don't know. We've got to talk about it. Christ, we've got to talk about it."

Six Years Earlier

"Jo, look at this," Miles says, and gives her a photograph that he's brought home from the university. The photograph shows a fractured yellow skull sitting in dirt.

Joanna says, "Is it significant, Miles?"

"Very," Miles answers. "She was apparently someone quite special, judging from the artifacts we found buried with her. But she was buried outside the common burial area, and we don't understand why."

C.J., standing nearby, tugs at Miles's pant leg. "What is it, sport?" Miles asks. "That time already?" He looks at his watch. C.J. has to be at nursery school in fifteen minutes.

C.J. nods and says, "Can Mommy take me?"

"Sure," Miles tells him. "I've got to get to school, anyway." He takes the picture of the skull back from Joanna, puts it in his briefcase and says, "This is causing quite a stir, let me tell you."

"Stir?" C.J. says.

Miles leans over and hugs him, then kisses Joanna lovingly, and long. He sees C.J. looking, gets red in the face and says, "Be a good boy, C.J. I love you," and goes to school.

SEVENTEEN

WHAT HAPPENED THE DAY
AARON GOT LOST

And now I don't think there was any little black dog. I think I *put* him there, and I think I put some other things there, too, like the woman with a green dress who was carrying a J.C. Penney's box and wearing rings, and also the man with the T-shirt that said *Shit Happens*.

"But I see all of these things as if they are real in my memory. Just like I see Dad and Mom and Aaron, who I know are real. So maybe they're real, too. But I don't think so. It's very bothersome. They're almost like *reflections* of real things, like when my father said to me and Aaron, 'If I face you and I hold up my right arm and I say, "You be my mirror image," which arm would *you* hold up?' And I said, 'My left arm,' and Dad smiled, like he was putting something over on me, or playing a trick on me, and he said, 'Then when you look into a mirror is it the left arm of the reflection that raises?' And when I thought about this for a moment I said, 'No, it isn't.' But I didn't know why it wasn't, because it was true that it would be *my* left arm, but the reflection's *right* arm, and I didn't know why. And

Dad explained to me, 'Because what you're seeing in a mirror is only an *image,* not a real person, not *you.* Do you understand? It, that reflection, has no right or left arm, it is only the *image* of *your* right and left arms.' But I didn't understand then because I was only six years old, and that's what I think when I look at the memory of the black dog and the man with the *Shit Happens* shirt, that it is only like an image in a mirror.

"Maybe I put it there to cover up what really happened.

"And I wonder why there was a black dog. I didn't see a black dog. But I *remember* seeing a black dog, and I remember, three years and seven months ago, seeing Marie in her bedroom when Dad wasn't home, and she was naked and I walked by the door, which was open, and she was looking at me. She was smiling. It was a gross smile. It was crooked. And her lips were awfully red. Her skin was sort of dark, sort of red-brown, and I had not seen her look like that before. And her lips were full of lipstick or something, and they were very red."

Miles repeated, "Lorraine, *what* happened to you last night?"

She shook her head, but said nothing. Her gaze was on the bedroom ceiling.

"You're not going to tell me what happened to you?" Miles coaxed.

"There's nothing . . ." She looked at him. "I don't know what there *is* to tell you, Miles. If I . . . made something up, it would be just as credible as . . ." She sighed, looked at the ceiling again, and continued, in a rush, "I went outside last night, and there were no houses there, no lights, no any-thing. Just . . . trees. Lots of trees, and stars. And people, too, I think. I saw . . . someone moving in the dark . . ." She looked intently at him. "Miles, I touched one of the trees—my God, I *had* to touch *something!* I had to find out how . . . *real* everything was. And I touched the tree, I felt it, I felt the bark . . . And my hand went . . . into it." She shook her head and looked away again. "Then I was . . . then the houses were back, and the lights. And everything else." She gave a trembling sigh.

"Christ," Miles said, "I'm sorry."

"You're sorry? For what?"

He looked befuddled. "I don't know. It just came out. I guess . . . I think I meant that I was sorry you were so . . . scared. I imagine you were very scared. It must have been disorienting, something like that, that kind of weird illusion . . ."

"I touched it, Miles. I touched the tree and it was *real!*"

"No," Miles corrected her. "You said that your hand went through it. So, how real could it have been?" He smiled nervously. "Try putting your hand through a real tree, Lorraine. It's very difficult." His nervous smile increased.

"Damn you, Miles, you're laughing at me!"

He shook his head quickly. "I'm not laughing at you. Believe me. It's just not possible . . . any of this—" He stopped, averted his gaze.

"Any of what, Miles?"

He looked at her again and feigned a confused expression. "What you told me, of course. It's not possible. Some things are possible, some very strange things. Mice with two heads, for instance. That's possible, I've seen it, in fact. And men who grow to be eight feet tall. But not what you told me. That's not possible, Lorraine, and I believe that, if you think about it—"

"You're babbling, Miles. You're acting like a fool."

He nodded. "Yes, I know. I'm sorry." He looked away, looked back, added, "What did you mean when you said you didn't know Marie?"

She gave him a long, quizzical look: *Why the abrupt change of subject?* the look said. She told him, "I don't remember saying that."

"Well, you did say it."

"Why *would* I say it, Miles?"

He shrugged. "I don't know. That's why I'm asking."

She looked at the ceiling. "Where were you last night?" She was suddenly angry.

He stared at her for a long moment. Her attitude puzzled him. "I was in jail," he said flatly.

"In jail? Why the hell were you in jail?"

"Because I was looking for Aaron. I was at the Triphammer Mall—I thought he might have been hiding there."

"You thought he was hiding at the mall for *two weeks?*"

Miles shrugged. "I thought it was possible. Christ, I was desperate, Lorraine."

"And you were caught there?"

"Yes."

She continued staring at him. Finally, sighing, she said, "I understand. I'm sorry," and she looked away.

"And I'm sorry I worried you," Miles said.

"I had a hell of a night," she whispered. She gave a flat smile—not at Miles, but at the ceiling—as if she had made a gross understatement. She stopped, shook her head. "I feel like shit, Miles. I had an awful night and I feel like shit."

He was put out by what she was saying. *He* was the one who had had an awful night. *He* was the one who had had to spend sleepless hours in a dingy jail cell on a hard and lumpy mattress. *He* was the one who had reason to feel like shit. He said, without conviction, "I'm sorry. Really," and began to undress.

She said, "What are you doing?"

He shrugged out of his shirt. "I was awake all night. I'm going to try and sleep now." He unbelted and unzipped his pants, took them off, got into bed next to Lorraine.

She said, gaze on the ceiling, "Are they pressing charges?"

"No one's pressing charges," he answered wearily. "They were very understanding."

"Good for them," Lorraine said.

Miles said nothing.

Lorraine said, after a long moment, "Something very odd is happening, Miles." She turned her head to look at him.

He nodded a little; she wasn't sure how to interpret it. His eyes were closed. He looked completely wiped out. "Do you agree?" she said.

"I agree."

Eighteen Months Earlier

"I'm going out now," Marie says. "Don't miss me. I'll be back."

Miles says, smiling, "I'll wait up for you." C.J., standing nearby, wonders why his father is smiling.

Marie smiles back. C.J. doesn't like her smile. He has never liked her smile.

She looks at C.J. and says to Miles, "Could you see that he's in bed when I get back, Miles?"

Miles looks at C.J., then at Marie. "Sure," he says.

As C.J. and Miles watch, Marie leaves the house, goes

down the porch, across the lawn to the driveway, gets into the car, shuts the door, starts the car.

C.J. says to Miles, "Our car needs a muffler. We haven't had a new muffler on it for a long time. Since three years ago, September second."

Miles smiles down at C.J. and says, "What do I need maintenance records for when I've got a kid like you around?"

"You don't need 'em, Dad," C.J. says. "I remember everything."

"Tell me about it," Miles says, and pats C.J. on the rear end. "Go on up and get ready for bed now, okay? I'll be up in a few minutes."

C.J. goes upstairs and gets ready for bed.

An hour later, when Miles has failed to come up and say good night, C.J. goes downstairs, finds him in the living room, and says, "I'm ready for bed, Dad."

Miles nods quickly, clearly upset. "Okay," he says. "Go on up, now. I'll tuck you in directly."

"Is Marie still at the store?" C.J. asks.

Miles nods quickly again. "Go upstairs, sport," he says. "Go on up, now."

"She's been gone a long time, Dad," C.J. says. "Why has she been gone so long?"

The phone rings and Miles goes across the living room and answers it. "Marie?" he says. "I don't understand. Where are you?" and, "What does *that* mean?" and, "Are you in some kind of trouble, Marie?" and, "Wait there. I'll get a cab. We'll talk about this," and, "What do you mean we can't talk about it? My God . . ." and "Dammit! Marie? Marie?" Then he hangs the phone up and looks earnestly at C.J., who's standing at the bottom of the stairs in his Huckleberry Hound pajamas. "Go get your brother," Miles says. "We have to go out."

"But Marie has the car," C.J. says.

"I *know* that!" Miles snaps.

And C.J. goes and gets Aaron up and helps him put on his clothes—Osh Kosh blue jeans and a white short-sleeved shirt, Yogi Bear sneakers, and green socks—and they go downstairs.

Miles is waiting for them at the open front door. "Here's the cab now," he says, and they all go out, get into the cab, and it takes them to the Stop 'N' Go that Marie goes to when she wants something to eat at night. But she isn't there.

Miles tells the cabdriver to wait, gets out of the cab, goes into the Stop 'N' Go, talks to the cashier, then returns to the cab and tells the cabbie to take them home.

Two hours later there's a phone call from the city police department: "Yes," Miles says into the receiver, "that's my wife," and "Yes, I'll bring one," and "Where?" and "I'll be there in twenty minutes." Then he calls up the cab company again, and the same cabdriver picks them up and takes them to a park nearby. Miles's car is there; its doors are open. Police are everywhere.

A plainclothes cop comes up to Miles and asks if he's brought a photograph of Marie, as has been requested. Miles pulls a three-year-old snapshot of Marie out of his jacket pocket and gives it to the cop.

"Did she say where she was going, Dr. Gale?" the cop asks.

"No," Miles answers. "She only said that she had . . . that she had had all the time she needed."

The cop says, "All the time she needed, Dr. Gale?" He

writes in his notepad. "Do you have any idea what that means?"

Miles shakes his head. "No, I don't."

"Did she sound confused, Dr. Gale? Disoriented?"

"If you're asking if she sounded *drunk,* no. Marie doesn't drink. I don't either."

"Not at all?"

"An occasional beer, or wine. That's it."

"Has she been depressed, suicidal?"

"Hell, no!"

"And that was all she said? That she was—" He checks his notepad.

"That she had had all the time she needed," C.J. offers.

The cop looks at him, face pinched in annoyance. Then he says to Miles, "Yeah, that she 'had had all the time she needed'?"

"Yes," Miles answers. "That was all she said." He hesitates. "It may have been that what she actually said was that she *had* all the time she needed."

The cop is confused. "Sorry. What's the difference?"

"The difference is one 'had' or two. The difference is past or present. I can't remember what she said exactly. She might have said that she 'had' all the time she needed, or 'had had' all the time she needed. There's a difference—"

"Yes sir," the cop interrupts, obviously skeptical.

"A big difference, really," Miles says.

"I don't see that there is," the cop says, and glances at the snapshot that Miles had given him. "We'll need something a little better than this, Dr. Gale. It's a bit fuzzy, don't you think."

EIGHTEEN

When Miles woke, it was dusk, and Lorraine was not in the bed with him. It was 5:45. He'd slept for nine hours, several hours longer than usual.

He sat up. "Lorraine?" he called.

After a moment, she called back, "I'm downstairs, Miles."

"Oh," he murmured, and fell back into the bed, suddenly weary. *Too much sleep,* he told himself. *Too many dreams.*

He remembered one dream particularly well:

He was in an old black-and-white movie; he was hanging from the hands of a huge clock. And the director, shouting at him through a bullhorn from far below, was saying, "Go ahead, fall, dammit. Fall!"

And he—Miles—shouted back, "I can't! I won't!" over and over again, in a panic.

And the director shouted, "But you have to. Don't you realize that? If you want to see him again, you have to fall! Now do it!"

In the dream, Miles began to weep because he realized that he had no choice but to let go of the hands of the clock. Soon, they'd be pointing downward, anyway, and he wouldn't be able to hang on any longer.

So, weeping, he let go.

And he fell for what seemed like weeks. He saw the sun rise and traverse the sky, saw it set, saw darkness come, saw the dawn over and over again. He witnessed the passing of days—saw *time* happening.

Then it all stopped.

He awakened.

And wondered where Lorraine was.

She called now, "Are you coming down? I made us some dinner."

He nodded, though she couldn't see the nod—he was still on his back in bed. He thought that he had never felt so overwhelmingly weary, as if he were a century old.

He wondered what he had seen the previous night. In the mall.

Marie?

"I did not know Marie," Lorraine had said. What had she meant by it? Simply that their long years of friendship had not been able to reveal the *real* Marie to her; that Marie, after all those years, was still a stranger to her? Perhaps. It seemed reasonable.

No, it didn't. He'd heard something else in Lorraine's voice. Something other than, *How well can you know anyone? How well could I have known Marie?*

He'd heard, "I did not know Marie." A bald and alarming statement of fact. "I did not know Marie."

"Miles, will you please come down. Dinner's getting cold."

He nodded again, flat on the bed; his weariness even made breathing difficult.

WHAT HAPPENED THE DAY
AARON GOT LOST

"There were trees and they were all around. I know about trees. I have studied trees and I've read lots of books about them. The trees around us there were of many kinds, but mostly they were northern white pine, and spruce and hemlock, maple, tulip tree, too. This is what is called a deciduous forest.

"All of these trees were very tall and this told me that it was an old forest. There were no young trees. Perhaps there were but I don't remember. The trees were so tall and there were so many of them the forest was dark, like it was almost night, but I could see some blue sky here and there through the tops of the trees. And there was the sun, too, right above, so I thought that maybe it was noontime.

"This was after Marie took Aaron, and I had gotten out of the car.

"And Dad said, not to me, but to no one, while he was still sitting in the front seat, with his window open, 'My God, what *is* this place? Where *are* we?'

"And I whispered to him, because I was very afraid, and I didn't know what might be listening, or who, 'It's the woods, Dad.'

"But I don't think that he heard me."

Miles seated himself at the dinner table. Lorraine had dressed in an ankle-length green dress and had done her long red hair up in a bun. She brought a plate of french fries, hot dogs, and peas to Miles, then got her own plate and sat at the opposite end of the table with it. "Want something to drink?" she asked.

"No," he answered. "Actually, I'm not hungry." He picked up his hot dog—it was covered with relish and mustard and wrapped in a slice of whole wheat bread the way he liked it—and gave it a nibble. It was satisfying to his tongue, which surprised him, so he took a bigger bite, then another.

"I thought you weren't hungry," Lorraine said.

"I wasn't," he said, and took several quick bites of the hot dog. Soon, it was gone. "Any more of those?"

Lorraine nodded. "You want me to get one for you?"

Miles shook his head. "No, it's all right."

She stood, said, "I'll get it," went to the stove, prepared him another hot dog, and brought it over.

"Thanks," he said, and began to devour it.

"I haven't seen you eat this much since . . ." She faltered.

He looked at her. "Since Aaron disappeared?"

"Yes," she said.

He continued looking at her for a few moments, then began eating again. Eventually, he stopped and said, "What did you mean when you said you didn't know Marie?"

She looked miffed. "I told you, Miles—I don't remember saying that. I was asleep."

"You mean it was something you were dreaming?"

"Probably."

"You don't remember?"

"I don't remember."

He looked at her a moment, then he asked, "Want some coffee?"

"When I'm finished eating," she answered. "Thanks."

He got up, began making coffee in the percolator, and said over his shoulder, "Marie was your friend for a long time before I met her, isn't that right?"

"Miles, why do you need to even ask?"

"When did you meet her?" He poured water into the percolator while she answered. He said, when he was finished pouring, "Sorry, I didn't hear you."

"I said that I met her in college. You knew that."

He nodded. "When you were what?—a sophomore?"

"Yes."

He plugged the percolator in. It began grumbling immediately, a fast percolator.

"A sophomore," he said. "You're sure?"

"Yes, of course I'm sure."

"You don't sound sure."

"C'mon, Miles. You might as well ask if I'm sure what city I grew up in, or how many brothers and sisters I have."

He got their favorite coffee mugs—cream-colored, restaurant-style mugs—from the cupboard above the percolator, set them on the counter, stared at the percolator, which was still perking, *glub, glub, glub.*

"Listen," Lorraine said, "I met Marie when I was nineteen years old, when I was a sophomore in college. It was . . . winter, I think. Late winter. Maybe early spring. It could have been March or April. I don't remember for sure. It was the month my brother got married, I know that. Hell, I invited her to come with me to the wedding."

"She didn't go?" Miles asked.

The coffee was still percolating, but it was percolating very fast, now—*gluba-gluba-gluba;* it was nearly done.

Lorraine shrugged. "I don't remember if she went with me or not."

Miles looked confusedly at her. "You don't remember? How could you not remember something like that?"

"Miles, give me a break." She looked stonily at him. "It was thirteen years ago. Some memories fade over time."

"Yes, I know."

"Well, they do."

"I didn't mean to upset you," he said.

"You haven't," she said, in a tone that clearly stated the opposite.

The coffee was done.

WHAT HAPPENED THE DAY
AARON GOT LOST

"And it was very quiet there all of a sudden, when I got out of the car.

"The wind stopped. It was a really strong wind. It made a noise high up in the trees that was like blowing into an empty bottle. But it stopped all of a sudden when I got out of the car. Then there were no sounds. There should have been some sounds. Birds, especially. But there weren't. There was no wind and there weren't any birds. So when my dad said, 'My God, where *are* we? What *is* this place?' and he was just whispering, I heard him like he was whispering into my ear. But I was outside the car. I was a couple feet from it. More, maybe. And the ground was squishy, like there was lots of water in it. I looked down and the ground was a sort of rust color.

"I yelled out to my brother, 'Aaron?' I couldn't hear anything. I couldn't hear my voice. Only a little. Like I was *thinking* 'Aaron?'

"And I began to get scared. I wasn't really scared till then. I don't know why. When I look back and remember, I still don't know why. Only that maybe it seemed like I was really just *thinking* the whole thing, the forest, and Marie, and Aaron disappearing. But then I got scared because I knew that it was real, or *looked* real, and that it wasn't supposed to *be* real.

"You know, if a glass of milk falls off a table, it goes *splat* on the floor and makes a mess. But if it does anything else, then it means that the universe is a topsy-turvy place, not the kind of universe you always thought it was.

"That's why I got scared. *Real* scared, so scared that my eyes began to blur and I couldn't breathe. And I jumped back in the car.

"And Dad said, 'What *is* this place?' Then I looked at him and his eyes were very wide, and he was staring through the windshield at all the green darkness around, all the forest.

"I said to him, 'Aaron's gone.' But he didn't look at me.

"I put my head way down, toward my lap, and my hands over my face, and I wished very hard that all the trees around the car would disappear.

"And they did."

NINETEEN

I n the bathtub at the Podkomiters', C.J. was thinking
that Marie never covered herself up when she was naked
and he was around. Lorraine did. Even his dad did. And
his mother, too. But not Marie.

She seemed to like being naked, in fact. C.J. supposed
that there was nothing wrong with that. Sometimes he liked
to not have any clothes on, too. He wished, when he was
swimming, for instance, that he could just shuck his swimming trunks, which were baggy and which seemed to fall off
his lean body from the weight of the water anyway. And, of
course, he liked having no clothes on when he was in the
bathtub. He thought his body was interesting. It had been
interesting to watch it grow and change over the years. He
could remember what it looked like when he was very small,
eighteen months old, he thought, when it was round and
pink and you could hardly tell that he was a boy unless you
looked close. But now he was eleven years old—much bigger, and harder, leaner, and meaner. And someday he'd be
a man. And there were times when he liked being naked.

Marie liked being naked at odd times. In the middle of
the day when she was making lunch for him and Aaron, for
instance, and his dad was at school. Or when she was giving
Aaron a bath. She wouldn't get in the bathtub with him—

C.J. couldn't remember if she had ever taken baths; she took showers, he supposed, though he couldn't remember that, either—but she would take her clothes off and hang them in the bathroom and wash Aaron while she was naked and the bathroom door was open.

She didn't like closed doors, C.J. remembered. If she came into the kitchen from outside and the door to the living room was closed, she would open it right away. She insisted that the bedroom door be kept open, even while she and C.J.'s dad were making love, which, C.J. thought, was a lot. She kept all the doors in the house open, even the closet doors. But she kept the front door and the back door locked, and the windows, too, even on hot days. And even on very hot days, C.J. remembered, she would not turn on the air conditioning. She seemed to like the heat, a lot more than *he* did, anyway. Aaron liked the heat, too.

"Are you just about through in there, young man?" Irene Podkomiter called, and rapped sharply on the door. C.J. scowled at the door. Dammit, he had gotten in here only eight minutes ago. Why couldn't she let him have some time to himself?

"Just a couple more minutes," he called back.

"Two minutes," Irene insisted. "You've been in there quite long enough to get yourself clean. And why do you lock this door? It's not good for little boys to be in the bathtub for too long alone."

What in the Sam hell does that mean? C.J. wondered.

He grimaced. "Okay," he called, "I'm getting out now."

There was no answer from the other side of the door. He had expected she would say something. She always liked to have the last word.

He pushed himself out of the tub and dried himself off

with a big yellow bath towel. It was soft and luxurious, and it felt good against his skin.

He called, "I'm getting out now," and glanced about the bathroom. It was small, functional. Not much to remember in it. A gleaming white sink standing on thin, stainless steel legs. The legs gleamed, too, though there were water spots on them here and there. The medicine cabinet over the sink was oak, and the mirror was cracked at the lower right-hand corner, just as he had remembered from his first visit to this room three days before.

The shower curtain, which was open, was white with a pastel orange and blue flower print. He looked at the curtain rod, then the curtain rings. Two of the rings were missing. That was as he remembered, too.

The bathtub was modern. There were a few rust stains near the drain, and there were blue, white, and yellow flower ring decals on the bottom of the tub to keep people from slipping when they were taking a shower.

The tub's faucet dripped. It dripped all the time; it needed a new washer, C.J. guessed.

The overhead light was a frosted globe with a long silver chain hanging from it.

A yellow wicker hamper stood to the left of the sink. The lid of the hamper was propped open a bit because of the full load of clothes inside.

All just as he had unconsciously committed to his amazing memory—three days ago.

He didn't even need to look, he thought. It was all in his head.

Heck, he could go blind, and as long as he was in a place he'd seen only once, it would be all right.

It was *all in his head.*

"I'm coming out," he called. Something scraped against the other side of the door.

"Huh?" he whispered.

Irene Podkomiter rapped sharply on the bathroom door again. "I want you *out* of there this instant, young man, is that clear?"

She got no answer, so she rapped again, even more sharply. "You answer me, C.J., or, by God, I'll know the reason why."

Carl Podkomiter—still dressed in his boxer shorts, T-shirt and socks—stuck his head out into the hallway and called, "What the hell's the problem, Irene?"

She glanced at him, her broad face livid with anger. "This *boy* is not answering me. He's got the goddamned door locked and he's not answering me."

Carl came out into the hallway. "C.J.?" he called.

C.J.'s fingers relaxed and the big yellow bath towel slipped to the floor. A shiver ran through him. He picked up the towel, wrapped himself in it.

"Hello?" he called. "Is someone there?"

The scraping noise on the other side of the door continued.

"Mrs. Podkomiter?" he called. "Mr. Podkomiter?"

The scraping noise continued. It was low, rasping, barely audible, like a whisper.

C.J. stared at the door. It was white and there was a black clothes-hook in the middle of it. His blue jeans hung from the hook, and his white shirt, too. Here and there some of the cream-colored paint had chipped, revealing the black paint beneath. This was true around the edges of the door, especially.

The bathroom floor was damp from water that had fallen from C.J. when he had gotten out of the tub.

The tub faucet still dripped.

Carl Podkomiter knocked on the bathroom door. "C.J., open up, okay?"

Nothing.

"Dammit!" Carl breathed. He felt above the door for the key. There was a hole in the middle of the knob; opening the door was simply a matter of putting the pointed key in the hole. But the key wasn't above the door. "Where *is* it?" Carl whispered.

"Wait a minute," Irene said, went to the bedroom, and came back moments later with a knitting needle in hand. "Use this," she said.

He tried to open the door with it. "It's too big. It doesn't fit," he said. "Get me a smaller one, okay?"

She nodded, took the knitting needle from him, went back to the bedroom, and reappeared momentarily with a thinner needle. "This is a number eight. It's smaller," she said, and handed it to him. It fit in the hole in the doorknob, but the door still didn't open.

"You've got to get it just right," Irene said. "You can feel the lock if you're careful."

C.J. knew what the rasping noise sounded like, now. He had heard it on TV, and at the movies, although never in real life. It was the branch of a tree rubbing against the door.

He shook his head. *Go away!* he thought. *Please, please go away!*

He took a couple of steps back, felt the butt of his heel

hit the tub, felt himself falling backward and lurched forward, regaining his balance.

The ceiling light was on.

The ceiling light is on! he thought. *The ceiling light is on, the ceiling light is on!*

So, what he supposed was at the other side of the door could not *be* at the other side of the door because the *light* was *on.*

It was simple. He was connected to the house, to the utility company, to the city, to the rest of the world as it was. *His* world. The modern world.

Because the ceiling light was *on!*

He smiled, relieved. He reached, pulled the chain for the light.

The light stayed on.

Marie had said once, "What a wonderful memory you have. You don't even need to *see,* really, do you? It's all right up there, everything"—and she tapped his forehead; her finger was cold—"the whole world."

He screamed now, "Help me! Somebody help me!"

The ceiling light went out.

TWENTY

Miles said into the phone, "What do you mean he's missing?"

Carl Podkomiter, on the other end of the line, stammered, "He was in . . . the bathroom . . . he couldn't have gone anywhere—" Carl paused. "But, my God, when we opened the door—he'd locked the door, and he wouldn't answer us, so we had to get a key and open the door, and when we did he . . . just wasn't there. We don't know where he went."

"Have you called the police?"

"Yes. They're on their way. Irene said I shouldn't call you, but you're the boy's father, after all, and to tell you the truth, Dr. Gale—"

"Could he be hiding somewhere in the house?"

"We've looked," Carl answered. "Everywhere. The cellar, the attic, the bedrooms . . . He isn't *here*. And we've looked outside, too. Irene is still looking. She's got a flashlight and she's out there calling to him. Hear her?"

There was a moment's silence, then Miles heard, very distantly, "C.J.? Answer me!" Carl came back on the line. "As soon as I hang up, Dr. Gale, I'll—"

"Yes," Miles interrupted, "keep looking. He's probably around the house somewhere."

"We were thinking that he might be on his way back there, to his own house."

Miles nodded at the phone. "That's possible, isn't it." He put his hand over the mouthpiece and said to Lorraine, standing nearby, "Get my coat for me," and nodded to indicate the kitchen closet. He took his hand away from the mouthpiece and said, "Give me your address, Mr. Podkomiter. I'll be there as soon as I can."

Carl gave Miles his address.

"Good," Miles said. "I'll be there in fifteen minutes."

When he was halfway to the Podkomiters' house, a rain started. The horizon ahead was clear; fading sunlight had painted it a deep brown and red. Miles hoped, seeing this, that the rain was only an early December aberration and that it would end quickly. "Good Lord," he whispered, "I'm going to be looking for my son in the dark in the rain."

Six Years Earlier

C.J. gets up and pees, then goes and looks into his mother and father's room, sees his father sleeping, and knows that his mother is downstairs because he can hear her moving around in the kitchen.

He hears two voices from below. Women's voices. One is his mother's and the other is hard to listen to because it's harsh and angry. "Mommy?" he calls from the top of the stairs. But there is no answer.

He listens for a minute to the voices from downstairs. Then there is silence. "Mommy?" he calls again, but still there's no answer.

He goes back to his mother and father's bedroom and

sees that his father is beginning to rouse from sleep, but isn't yet awake enough that C.J. can talk to him.

He goes back to the top of the stairs and hesitates, suddenly fearful, though he isn't sure why.

He hears now that the radio is playing in the kitchen. Classical music—his mother's usual morning fare. He hears a truck stop in front of the house. Monday morning garbage pickup.

"Morning, sport," he hears, and turns his head to see his father leaving the bathroom. C.J. says nothing. He continues down the stairs.

The radio announcer says, "That was Mozart's *Prelude in G,* Kerschel listing 112."

Miles calls from the bedroom, "Jo, have you put the coffee on? I've got to get to the school right away."

C.J. continues down the stairs one slow step at a time.

The radio announcer says, "Coming up next, 'Morning Edition.' "

"Jo? Coffee?" Miles calls.

C.J. sees his mother's red slipper on the cream-colored kitchen floor. *Something's wrong,* he thinks and begins to cry because of his fearful uncertainty.

"Jo," Miles calls, "you downstairs? Jo? Have you put the coffee on?"

"Mommy?" C.J. whimpers. He's only a few steps from the bottom of the stairway, now. "Can I have Maltex?" he says. It's a way of telling himself that everything is all right. His mommy isn't hurt. She will make him Maltex, as she always does.

Hugh Vinikoff said to Miles, when Miles came into the Podkomiters' living room, "How did you get this address, Dr. Gale?"

Miles said nothing for a moment, uncertain how to respond, and Carl Podkomiter said, "I told him. I thought he should know that C.J. was missing. He's the boy's father, after all."

Vinikoff digested this for a moment, then nodded sullenly. "Sure," he said. "It's all right. Actually, Dr. Gale, I'm glad you're here. C.J. will probably come to you first. In fact, that's probably where he went, back to his own house."

"Yes," Miles said, "I've thought of that."

"Is anyone there?" Vinikoff asked.

Miles nodded. "Yes. Someone's there."

Vinikoff said, "I think I'll call to have a car sent over, anyway." He looked questioningly at Carl Podkomiter, who said, "The telephone's in the kitchen."

Vinikoff went into the kitchen.

Carl, looking very embarrassed, said, "I'm sorry, Dr. Gale. We had no idea he'd leave the house. At night especially."

"I understand that," Miles said. Then, glancing about the small, simply furnished living room, "Your wife is still looking?"

"No," Carl answered. "She's upstairs, lying down. This whole thing has gotten her very upset." He paused, then hurried on apologetically, "But she looked for C.J. a very long time, Dr. Gale. Since before I called you. And she got the neighbors to look, too, which, in this neighborhood, was quite a trick, let me tell you—"

Detective Vinikoff reappeared from the kitchen. He took a breath. "Your boy's been found, Dr. Gale," he said.

Miles looked silently at him a moment. *Which boy?* he wanted to ask. But Vinikoff came forward, cupped Miles's elbow in his hand, and went on, "If you could come with me, please."

WHAT HAPPENED THE DAY
AARON GOT LOST

"Once, a long time ago, Dad took me to the school where he works, down into the basement, where they keep the bones that they work on. It's very cool in the basement at the school. Dad likes to work down there.

"The bones are on many, many floor-to-ceiling shelves, and a lot of them are still in the dirt that they were found in. This dirt is in boxes made of pressure-treated wood. Dad says that they move the bones in the dirt, sometimes, so they won't disturb the way the bones were put into the ground. He says that the way the bones were put into the ground (and actually they weren't just bones then, they were usually whole bodies), the way they were put into the ground indicates something about them, their place in the tribe, or whatever. Plus, if you take the bones out of the ground you might miss something small and leave it at the site where the bones were.

"I was five then, when Dad took me into the basement at the school. I remember mostly how cool and dark it was. There were lights but they weren't very bright and the hallways in the basement were narrow and not very tall, especially for my dad, who's six feet two and almost hit the ceiling. I was only four feet, and I didn't have to bend over.

"The ceiling didn't seem short, then, but when I look at it now, in my memory, it does.

"There was another archaeologist down there in the basement. His name was Dr. Sam Burford, and Dad introduced me to him. 'This is my son, C.J.,' said my dad, and Dr. Burford took a couple of steps toward me. He bent over and smiled (he smelled of tobacco and I saw a pipe sticking out of his jacket pocket) and said, 'Well, how do you do, young man?'

"I said, 'I'm doing fine.' I shook his hand. It was soft and it felt a little gritty because he had been working with bones in one of the boxes when we came into the room. There were many rooms in the basement of the school and not all of them were for the storage of bones. Some of them had books and file cabinets and desks and papers bound up with twine and wastebaskets and many odds and ends.

"Dr. Burford said, 'What do you think of this place, C.J.? Kind of spooky?'

"I shook my head and said, 'No, it isn't.'

"He seemed disappointed by this and he stopped smiling for a moment. But then he smiled again right away, and said, 'Well, it's good that you don't think it's spooky, C.J. Maybe someday you'll be down here working with us.' His smile got bigger as if he liked what he had said. He was older than my dad, and very fat. His stomach bulged out and almost hit me in the forehead when he straightened up. I took a step backward, away from him, and he looked at my dad and said, 'That skull from site twenty-four is yielding some surprises, Miles. Come have a look.'

"My dad held out his hand to me and I reached up and took it. 'Come on, sport,' he said.

"And we went and looked at the skull that Dad had brought home pictures of.

"I couldn't see anything, though. Not at first. The box that the skull was in was on a shelf that was above my head and I looked up at my dad and Dr. Burford while they talked about it. Dr. Burford took a pen from his pocket and pointed at the skull, I think, or some part of the skull, and he said, 'See this fissure, Miles? I thought at first that it was caused by an earlier wound, one that might have healed. It seemed likely. A skull fracture, I thought. But then I looked more closely. See here.'

"My dad bent over and looked at the skull while Dr. Burford got a little flashlight from his pants pocket and shone it at the skull. He said, 'Look at this. The fissure is echoed here, and here, and here. It's echoed quite precisely, Miles.'

"My dad said, 'That's damned odd.'

"Dr. Burford said, 'I thought so, too. I thought it was *fucking* odd, in fact.' He looked at me and said, 'Oops.' He grinned at me. His teeth were large. He said, 'Don't repeat that, C.J.'

"My dad said, 'It's no problem, Sam,' then said, 'This is almost a kind of wave effect, isn't it?'

" 'Sorry?' said Dr. Burford.

" 'Well, I mean, look at it,' said my dad. 'It looks like waves coming to shore.'

" 'That's fanciful,' said Dr. Burford. 'Not very scientific,' he said, 'but fanciful as hell.'

"I reached up and tugged at my dad's hand. 'Can I see?' I asked.

"He didn't answer me right away. He didn't hear me, I think. I guess he was too interested in the skull. But after a moment he said, 'Huh. Oh, sure, sport,' and reached down and picked me up so I could look at the skull.

"It was the same skull that was in the photograph that Dad had brought home, and it wasn't very white. I thought it would be as white as clouds. But it was yellow, like teeth that are dirty or never brushed. And there wasn't the whole skull, either. The jaw was missing. And it had the hole in the top of it that the skull in the picture had.

"It was sitting in the black dirt, and it seemed to be smiling, which I think now was strange because it didn't have a jaw, and it would be very hard to smile without one. But I thought it was smiling, then. And when I look at it with my memory, now, it's still smiling. This may have been because of the way the dirt was piled up at both edges of the lips, which were not there, of course, since it was only a skull, and not even a whole skull.

"And while I was looking at it, Dr. Burford said, 'I've made some measurements, Miles. They're unusual, too. Cranial capacity, diameter of the eye sockets, width of the upper jaw, everything is larger than normal.'

" 'She was a large person, no doubt,' said my father, and he reached down and put his hand on the skull, like he was putting his hand on *my* head, which he used to do a lot. And he rubbed that skull the same way he rubbed my head.

" 'Uh-huh,' said Dr. Burford.

"My dad put me down, then. 'You're getting pretty heavy, sport,' he said. He said that a lot. This was before he started doing his exercises, which he now does twice a day.

"Dr. Burford said, 'Well, the *size* of the eye sockets, et cetera, is not what is so unusual. It's the *symmetry* that's unusual, Miles.'

"My father said, 'Oh?'

" 'Yes,' said Dr. Burford. 'I've taken a number of measurements comparing both hemispheres of the skull. All of the measurements, left to right, are equal. They don't differ by even a millimeter.'

" 'Christ,' said my dad, 'that *is* fucking odd.'

"And I am talking about all of this now, even though it does not seem like a part of the stuff I should be remembering so we can get Aaron back, because I know that the skull that my dad was touching then was important, I think that it was Marie, and I think that that is the truth, and I don't think it matters that Marie was a person who was alive, because I don't think that Marie was a person at all. I think that she was something else.

"Once, I said this to my father, that Marie was not really a person. But he only looked at me and he had no expression on his face."

TWENTY-ONE

Room 603 of the psychiatric wing at Mercy Hospital was small, starkly furnished, and very warm. The thermostat controlling the whole wing wasn't working properly.

The doctor who had shown Miles, Lorraine and Detective Vinikoff into the room explained, "I'm told that the problem with the heat is only a temporary glitch. If it's not cleared up in half an hour, we'll move him."

C.J. lay on a twin bed between the room's one window and the wall farthest from the door. He was on his back. A gray blanket covered him to his neck, except for his bare arms, which were extended at his sides outside the blanket. His fists were clenched, and his eyes were wide and staring, apparently at nothing. He was strapped to the bed at his wrists and ankles.

Miles, Lorraine, and the detective stood silently just inside the doorway for several long moments. Then Miles whispered, "C.J.?" and started across the room. The doctor put a hand to Miles's chest and said, "If we could just let him rest a while, Dr. Gale, as we discussed."

Miles looked blankly at the man. "What could it hurt to let him know I'm here?"

"Doubtless, he *knows* you're here," the doctor answered. "He is, however, in a highly agitated state—"

Lorraine cut in, "He looks like he's in a coma."

The doctor shook his head. "No. He's not in a coma, Miss Rabkin. Far from it. We've given him some Demerol; it should help. He's a lot less agitated than when he was brought here, at any rate."

Miles called, his tone even and reassuring, "C.J.—it's me, it's Daddy. You'll be all right, sport." He looked pleadingly at the doctor. "Can I please just . . . let him *see* me, for Christ's sake!"

The doctor shook his head. "As I told you, he is doubtless aware of your presence in the room. That's his problem; he's aware of far *too* much. He's apparently being bombarded by stimuli." The doctor paused. "We really should leave now. Perhaps in an hour or so . . ."

C.J. screamed. It was the high-pitched and healthy scream of a young boy and it was ragged with panic.

"Dammit!" the doctor muttered.

Miles ran across the room to comfort his son.

WHAT HAPPENED THE DAY AARON GOT LOST

"It was a long time ago, and Dad was talking into a tape recorder. He did that a lot. He was reading from his notebook and talking into his tape recorder and there were pictures in front of him, on his desk, and the pictures were of the skull that he had found, and also of the places where he found other skulls and other skeletons. And this is what he said.

" 'The skeletons are heavy-boned, with strong muscular

attachment, and the heads are broad, round, and of medium height in the vault. Cranial capacity is good. The face is relatively short and wide and is characterized by a prominent lateral and anterior projection of the malars, medium to low orbits, and a short, broad nose.' Dad saw that I was watching him. 'What are malars?' I asked.

"He answered, 'Cheekbones, sport,' and he pointed at his cheekbones.

" 'Oh,' I said. 'Do *I* have cheekbones?'

" 'You sure do,' Dad said. And he reached out and touched my own cheekbones. I touched them.

"Dad smiled. Then he went on talking into his tape recorder. He said:

" 'All of the remains, except for the remains of the individual whose skull was located at grid three, were heavily pressure-fractured from the weight of the earth upon them. Twenty-two of these skeletons are in the process of restoration.

" 'It was obvious that the female skull found at grid three was not of the same group. The skull is of exceptional cranial capacity, certainly higher than the rest of the group, and is narrow, oval, and very high in the vault, with almost no eyebrow or temporal ridges. The skull is strikingly like that of the Lamoka people, although carbon dating, to about 4450 B.C., and its placement at the site, put it with the Frontenac Island Laurentian people. The malars are similar to the Frontenac Island people, however, although the nose is narrow, and long, as opposed to the broad, short noses which typify the rest of the group.

" 'It can only be assumed that this individual, with whom there were found several burial gifts, uncommon for women of the period—note, these gifts will be discussed later, as they, in and of themselves, are a point of interest—was a

visitor, though we have found no other Archaic evidence of
people similar to her.

" 'It is also evident that the skull was decapitated since
the articulated cervical vertebrae were still in place.'

"I said to my dad, 'What's decapitated?'

"He looked at me for a moment as if he didn't want to
answer, then he ran his finger across his throat and grinned
and said, 'It means you get your head cut off, sport.'

"I said, 'Somebody got their *head* cut off?'

"He nodded and said, 'Yep. This little lady here.' And he
showed me the picture of the skull again.

"I said, 'That's no lady.'

"He smiled, like he was thinking of something funny but
wasn't going to say it, then he said, 'Well, she *was* a lady,
sport. A long, long time ago.'

"I said, 'Like when you were little, Daddy?'

" 'Even before then,' said my dad. 'Even before your
grandma and grandpa were little, and even before *their*
grandmas and grandpas were little. Even before there was
a United States. Do you understand?'

"I shook my head. I didn't understand.

"My dad said, 'Of course you don't. Someday you will,
though. For now,' and he pointed at the skull in the picture,
'let's suffice it to say that this is the skull of a very early
American Indian, and that all of these other pictures are
also of very early American Indians. And these people lived
right around here, sport. Right around this house. That is,
before there *was* a house. Before there were *any* houses, in
fact. And these people lived around here even before the
people most people think of as Indians lived here. And you
know that the Indians were misnamed by a man named
Christopher Columbus, also a long time ago, who thought

that he had sailed to a place called India. Do you understand?'

"I shook my head.

" 'I thought not,' said my dad. But he seemed to be enjoying talking to me, because I always listened, because I always soaked everything up, which is something he used to say a lot, 'Soaking everything up, sport?' he used to say, and I used to nod and say, 'Soaking everything up, Dad.' He doesn't say that anymore. I miss him saying that. He thinks that it'll make me self-conscious or something. But it won't. I *know* that I'm different. But I'm not *really* different. I just remember everything. My brain is like some kind of tape recorder. Everything that goes in there stays in there. Sometimes it gets very confusing. Sometimes I wish all the stuff in there would go away.

"And my dad said, because he could see that I was listening real hard, and he liked to talk about the Indians, anyway, because, he told me once, he had some Indian blood in him, Blackfeet, he said, 'And all of these very early Americans, these first Indians, on this island, it's called Frontenac Island, now, sport, but who knows what the Indians called it, they didn't leave us anything written down—all these Indians died at about the same time, and they all died from the same thing. They all died from some kind of disease. It made their bones atrophy and turn rubbery, just like this pen,' and he took his pen, which was made of some plastic that was soft and could bend, and he bent it.

"He stopped talking and looked at me. I was crying. What he was telling me was very scary. I didn't want him to keep talking, but I knew he liked to talk about the Indians, so I didn't say anything, I just started crying, and he stopped talking. 'Sorry, sport," he said. "Sometimes I get carried away.'

"And I didn't understand very much then. But I do now. While I'm talking into this tape recorder. I understand a whole lot. I do. I understand about Marie and Aaron and everything. And I understand about the trees that were there at the mall. And about my mother, and about the skull—I think that I understand about the skull, like I said before. I think that I understand about it, and I don't think that I'm wrong.

"But who would believe me?"

TWENTY-TWO

Miles had unbuckled the straps holding C.J.'s wrists and now was hugging him, stroking his hair, rocking him back and forth in the bed.

He could feel that C.J. was fighting him. The boy's lean, small body was hard and tense, and he was shivering, as if from fear. But Miles could tell that C.J. didn't want him to let go, so Miles held him, fought him, comforted him. "It's okay, sport," he whispered. "Nothing's going to harm you. You've got nothing to worry about here."

C.J.'s doctor stood nearby, arms folded at his chest, mouth tight. He was clearly on the verge of some complaint, but he said nothing.

Miles asked him, "Did C.J. *say* anything when he was brought in, Doctor?"

The doctor nodded once. "Yes. He said 'Marie.' He said it a number of times, in fact. I've been told that that was your second wife's name."

"Marie, yes," Miles said.

"And that she disappeared a year ago. Is that correct?"

"Yes. Eighteen months ago, actually." Miles looked at C.J. He could see only the top of the boy's head; C.J.'s face was buried in Miles's chest. Miles looked at the doctor again. "Did my son say anything else?"

"Other than the name 'Marie,' no," the doctor answered. "I've yet to speak with the paramedics who brought him in, however."

"And where was he found?"

"On the southern expressway, about a mile from where he disappeared. He was naked, Dr. Gale. We had expected he'd be suffering from hypothermia, but there was no evidence of it. It's likely that his state of high agitation may have helped him to combat it. When he was located, he was running, and I'm told that he did not seem to be aware, at first, of the police who found him."

This is what C.J. remembered.

Everything.

The white bathroom door that was chipped here and there around the edges, revealing the black paint beneath.

The gleaming white sink that stood on thin, stainless steel legs. The water spots on the stainless steel legs. The oak medicine cabinet over the sink. The cracked mirror. The shower curtain, white with a pastel orange and blue flower print. The two missing curtain rings. Modern bathtub. Rust stains. The blue, white and yellow flower ring decals, the dripping faucet, the overhead light and frosted globe and long silver chain. The yellow wicker hamper overflowing with clothes.

The rasping noise from the other side of the door.

The door opening fast and hard, as if some powerful and angry animal had thrown it open.

The moonlit dark beyond.

The wind.

The people.

His father's words: "The skeletons are heavy-boned, with strong muscular attachment, and the heads are broad, round, and of medium height in the vault. Cranial capacity is good. The face is relatively short and wide and is characterized by a prominent lateral and anterior projection of the malars, medium to low orbits, and a short, broad nose."

The people . . . moving about in the moonlit dark, in the woods, in the wind, their naked bodies reflecting the creamy moonlight:

It was all he could see of them—the reflection of moonlight from their skin as they moved.

Muscular thighs and chests and torsos. Broad, short faces. Widely spaced eyes and high cheekbones reflecting the creamy moonlight.

Ghosts in the woods, in the wind, in the dark.

C.J. shivered violently. "No!" he murmured. "Go away!"

Miles held him tighter. "It's all right, C.J. No one's going to hurt you. It's all right."

C.J. heard him.

And he knew that it wasn't all right.

WHAT HAPPENED THE DAY
AARON GOT LOST

"My dad said, not to me, not to anyone, I think—he was sitting in his chair, and my mother's funeral was over just that day and she was buried—and he said to no one, even though I was sitting in the living room, too, 'Slowly, we all become shadows.' He whispered it, so I guess that he was saying it to himself.

"But I said it, too. 'Slowly, we all become shadows.' I didn't know what it meant. I do now.

"And he looked at me, back then, like he was surprised

by hearing my voice. And he said, 'Don't think about it, C.J. Don't dwell on it.'

"I said, 'Mommy's buried? Mommy's in heaven?'

"He nodded. He said, 'Go on up to your room, sport, okay?'

"I said, 'Okay,' and I went up to my room.

"I closed my door.

"I lay down on my bed, on my back, with my arms folded on my chest.

"I cried.

"I thought, *Mommy's buried!* and when I tried to remember her, I couldn't. I saw somebody else, somebody who looked like Mommy, somebody with dirt all over her, dirt getting into her mouth and eyes and nose, so she couldn't breathe.

"And something inside me said that she didn't *need* to breathe anymore.

"I screamed, 'Liar!'

"I heard a hissing noise in the room so I stopped my own breathing. The hissing noise stopped.

"Daddy was on the stairs, I thought. I could hear him on the stairs. He was coming up the stairs.

"It was a very bright day. And warm. The sun filled up my whole room with yellow sunlight.

"Daddy came down the hallway. It was a long hallway in that big house, the house where me and Mommy and Daddy lived.

"Daddy was talking into his tape recorder. He was saying, 'The Archaic, a term that denotes an early level of culture that was based on fishing, hunting, and gathering of wild vegetables, a culture that lacked pottery, agriculture, and the smoking pipe . . .'

"Daddy came down the hallway. It was a long hallway in

that big house, which was the house we lived in before we lived here. And the day was warm and bright, the sunlight filled my room up and made it very warm. I lay on my bed and I sweated.

"Daddy opened the door a little.

"He talked into his tape recorder, just like I'm talking into this one, now. 'The Robinson site covered some three acres of well-drained, nearly level terrace, fifteen to eighteen feet above the south shore of the lake. This occupied area was marked by a refuse mantle of black soil ten to thirty-two inches deep. Directly opposite, about a quarter mile away on the north bank of the lake, lay the Oberlander number one site, also on a level . . .'

"Then Daddy opened the door all the way.

"And the trees were there. In the doorway. Trees. Blue sky, too. And a blob of dark that floated about among the trees.

"The blob of dark touched the trees and stained them.

"It grew larger. It became more than a blob of dark. It became tall. It became the tall dark among the trees.

"And I remember now what my daddy whispered: 'Slowly, we all become shadows.'

"And the tall dark came through my doorway in that big house that we lived in a long time ago, before we lived in this house, but after my mom was dead, and before Marie was living with us, and that tall dark crossed the room in the sunlight, and the sunlight was gone because the tall dark ate it. Then the tall dark was beside my bed. And I said to it, 'Mommy?'

"And the tall dark leaned over my bed.

"And I said to it again, 'Mommy?'

"It hissed at me.

"And I screamed, 'Mommy! Mommy!'

"And the tall dark came over me like night and wrapped me up in itself and I felt very cold, and I screamed, 'Mommy! Mommy!'

"My daddy came in, then. He was there. Mixed up with the tall dark. Him and the tall dark together next to my bed so I couldn't see his face. And he bent over and said, 'Are you all right, sport?' His face was gone. The dark was there.

"And this is who the dark was, which I know now, but did not know then. The dark was Marie. It was Marie, somehow. The tall dark was *Marie* before she *was* Marie.

"And this is something that is true."

TWENTY-THREE

Miles and Lorraine left C.J. at the hospital and drove home, neither of them talking, not even when they went into the house and tried to decide if there would be any benefit in sleep. But they were both exhausted, so they went up to the bedroom, undressed, climbed into bed, and lay with their eyes open.

At last, Miles said, his voice ragged with a mixture of anger and frustration and sadness, "I feel like I'm coming apart, Lorraine." He emphasized "coming apart." He spat it.

She said, "I understand that."

"Do you?" he said. "Both of my sons are . . . gone. You can't imagine what that does to me—"

"I *can* imagine it, Miles. I can imagine it very well." She was scolding him. She could hear it in her voice. She didn't want to scold him because she really *did* know how he felt. She cared for Aaron and C.J., too. And he—Miles—had asked her to share his life, so she was sharing this awful time with him. It was unfair and thoughtless of him to suggest that she couldn't understand how he was feeling.

But she told him, anyway, "I'm sorry."

"It's very dark," he said.

"Is it?" She noticed that it was. "Yes, it is," she said, her voice quivering with unease.

He said, "Darker than it should be."

She said nothing.

He sat up in the bed and glanced about. He could see the room's furnishings—the tall chest of drawers, the white bookcase, the silver floor-standing lamp. But he saw all these things mostly from memory. Their vague, and vaguely shimmering outlines, by themselves, could have told him little had he not known what they were, and that was not as it usually was in the room at night. Usually, light from spotlamps and floodlights and security lights in the subdivision lit the room well enough to walk around in, even with the curtains closed, as they were now. But he thought he could not have walked around in this light.

"I don't like this," he said.

"Don't like what?" Lorraine said.

"It's too dark. It shouldn't be this dark."

"There's a cloud cover, Miles. It's nighttime. Of course it's dark."

"No," he said, clearly annoyed by her rationalizing.

He got out of bed and crossed slowly to the window.

He opened the curtain with one quick, sure pull on the cord.

And, with his face pressed hard into the cold window, and his hands cupped around the sides of his head, he peered out into the night.

He saw trees. They were tall and dark and very close. They crowded the house. They touched it. He could hear them touching it.

He shivered as fear grew inside him. His body tensed, his eyes watered, he felt cold, warm, cold.

Lorraine padded across the floor to where he stood and

put her hand on his arm and peered out, as he was doing. And she saw what he was seeing.

She straightened from the window. She shook her head quickly. "No!" she murmured.

He took her hand in the darkness. Her skin was cool. She gripped his hand very tightly.

They embraced. Each drew reality and reassurance from the caress of the other.

They embraced with their eyes closed. They embraced tremblingly.

And after many minutes, Lorraine whispered, into Miles's shoulder, again and again, "This is not real, this is not real!" while Miles hugged her very tightly, and she hugged him back, and they both reveled in the darkness because their eyes were closed, and because they knew— they were as sure of it as they were of their own names— that when they opened their eyes again they each would see the line of houses, the spotlamps and security lights and chain link fences that were a part of their existence here, in this last decade of the twentieth century.

They embraced each other for a very long time.

And when they opened their eyes, and looked, they saw that the trees still hugged close to the house.

Except there was gray light beyond them, now. Gray morning light winking through spaces between the dark trees.

And there were noises from below, too, in the first floor of the house, as if someone had come in and was moving stealthily about.

Miles whispered, "If this is . . . happening, Lorraine—" He took a deep, quivering breath and could say no more.

"But it's not," she protested.

"I think that it is," he said.

"Close the curtains, Miles. Please."

He nodded, reached tentatively for the curtain pull, grabbed it, gripped it very hard, and pulled the curtains shut.

"Thank you," Lorraine whispered.

"There's someone . . . downstairs," he whispered.

"No," she said.

"Yes," he said. "I've got to see who it is."

But she would not let go of him in the gray morning light. And he would not let go of her.

The noises from below stopped.

He glanced at the bedroom door. It was closed. *Is it locked?* he wondered. But why would it be locked? They were the only people in the house. There had been no need to lock the door. Neither C.J. nor Aaron was going to blunder in on them while they made love.

Lorraine said, "There *is* someone in the house, Miles. I can *feel* it." She took her arms from around his waist. They were sweaty. She put her hands flat on his chest, pushed away from him a little. He still had his arms around her; he relaxed, let her pull away. She pleaded, looking up at him and seeing little more of him in the gray early morning light than the oval of his face and the hollow of his eyes, "We'll keep the curtains closed, okay, Miles?"

He nodded at once. "Yes. There's no reason to open them. We'll keep them closed."

She nodded back. She said, "I don't think there's anyone in the house. I think I was mistaken. I was just . . . imagining it."

"We'll be quiet a moment," he said. "We'll listen."

She nodded.

They listened.

There was the noise of wind, leaves turning over.

He shook his head. "No one is in the house."

"No one," she said.

"We should . . . look," he said.

"Outside?"

"No," he answered at once. "No, I meant . . . in the house. We should look . . . we'll look in the house."

She nodded. He was easier to see, now. His eyes were bloodshot, she thought. She shook her head, put a finger to his lips; they were very dry, and very cool. His skin was pale; oddly, it was almost translucent. She said, "We are . . ." But she could say no more.

"Let's look in the house," he repeated.

She nodded.

But, instead, they stood quietly holding each other for many minutes.

And then she saw that sunlight was filtering through the dark curtains, turning his nearly translucent face rust-red.

She reached, touched the curtains where they met at the center of the window, fingered them, noted the feel of the heavy cloth.

Miles reached, took her hand. "No," he said. "Later."

She hesitated, withdrew her hand, nodded. "Yes. Later."

"We'll look in the house, first," he said.

She pushed farther away from him, so they were an arm's length apart. Sunlight painted his head and naked torso rust-red. The lower part of him, the part below the bottom of the window, was in semidarkness. His eyes were wide, disbelieving, bloodshot. He looked insane.

"We'll look now," she said, and turned at once from him and went very quickly to the door and opened it.

He watched her. Her back, her bare buttocks, her legs. Her body blocked his view of the open doorway and the hallway beyond.

"Do you see anything?" he called.

"The hallway," she called back. "There's nothing—" She stopped.

"Lorraine?" he coaxed.

She shook her head. She put her hands to the sides of the doorway, lowered her gaze.

"Lorraine?" he coaxed again.

The room was bright enough to read in. The sun had risen.

She turned abruptly, crossed the room in quick, long strides and threw the curtains open.

The light beyond was dark green. A forest.

She stared at it for a long moment.

Miles stared at her.

It occurred to him that they were both naked.

Lorraine whispered, "It is only an image."

"What?" Miles said. He hadn't heard her.

She glanced right, left, saw the lamp on the bedside table. She went to it, picked it up; it caught on the cord plugged into the wall. She yanked on the cord, freed it, went to the window. "It's only an *image,* dammit!" she shouted.

And she threw the lamp into the window.

The glass shattered.

Cool air rushed in, touched her, made goose bumps rise on her skin.

She screamed.

And Miles, with a quick and fearful glance into the dense, dark green forest beyond the shattered window, started toward her to comfort her.

But she turned and ran from the room, into the hallway.

He heard her moving down the stairs heavily, on her heels.

"Lorraine!" he called, and went after her.

WHAT HAPPENED THE DAY
AARON GOT LOST

"And the hissing noise was all around me, and I looked hard to see what was causing it, but I didn't see anything except the tall dark, and I remembered what my daddy said, 'Slowly, we all become shadows,' he said, and I whispered at the tall dark, 'Mommy?' But it was not my mommy and I knew it even then, I knew that the tall dark was something else, something evil, and I started to cry and to become afraid, and the hissing noise stopped. I heard, 'Everywhere. Everything. All time is mine.' It was not a woman's voice, and not a man's voice. It was the voice of air.

"And the tall dark was gone.

"My daddy was there.

"He said, 'Are you okay, sport?' I was crying.

"He leaned over me, like the tall dark had, and he didn't smell good, like he had been drinking whiskey, and this was the day my mom got buried. He said again, 'Are you okay, sport?'

"But I cried, and he comforted me by holding me, and I didn't mind the bad smell from him.

"And then it was five months later, in September, and we came home, after he picked me up at school, and he said, while he was driving me home, 'Lorraine is bringing someone over to meet me, sport. An old friend of hers, someone she knew from school. Someone named Marie. Isn't that a nice name? And we're going to make them both a real nice dinner, okay?'

"But I just looked at him and I didn't say anything.

"Then I was seven years old, almost eight, and Marie was talking to me, grinning at me. I was eating my lunch. Macaroni and cheese. Aaron sat in a high chair and he was eating, too. And Marie was grinning. Her face was real close to mine. She was leaning over and she smelled like the living room smells after Dad has made a big fire in the fireplace.

"Marie said to me, 'I remember so much more than you do, little man. What do *you* remember? Pissing your pants, falling down on the playground, babbling at your mother for more cereal. I remember so much more than that.

" 'I remember the *beginning,'* she said, still grinning at me. 'I remember *heat* and *light* and *wind!'*

"Then Aaron threw a big forkful of the macaroni and cheese at her. It hit her in the cheek. It stuck on her cheek for a moment, and then the pieces of macaroni slipped off on the floor. I thought it would make her angry. She got angry a lot. But she didn't get angry then. She didn't even seem to notice that Aaron had thrown a forkful of macaroni and cheese at her. She just kept on talking, with that yellow cheese on her cheek. And she was still grinning. She said, 'You could live a thousand years and remember every moment, every breath, every heartbeat, but it wouldn't mean a thing compared to what *I* remember. And you know the beauty of it, C.J.? The beauty of it is, you'll *never* know what I'm talking about.'

"Then she straightened up over the table and turned and faced Aaron, who was in his high chair, and she hit him hard with her hand across his cheek.

"But Aaron didn't cry. She had taught him not to cry. I thought it would be impossible to do, to teach a little kid not to cry when he got hit. But she did it."

TWENTY-FOUR

Six Years Earlier

M arie says, "Do you know what exists between *then* and *now,* my love?"

"Between 'then and now'?" Miles asks. "I don't understand."

She smiles coyly. It's a rare kind of smile from her. Her smiles are usually overtly sexual, cruel, or oddly childish. She answers, "Whatever *then* and whatever *now,* Miles. *That* then, and *this* now. Whatever you wish." Her coy smile grows playful. Then one corner of her full, very red lips lifts and her playful smile becomes a sneer.

"And what was the original question?" Miles asks. He's being playful now, and hopes that it will renew her playfulness.

Her smile vanishes. She cocks her broad head at him, as a child would. "Shadows," she says. "That's what exists between *then* and *now.* Get caught there, let the winds come and take you there, Miles, my love, and you'll see that I'm right. Only bright shadows against the light." She smiles again. "So much light. The light was first, you know. Then the darkness."

Miles smiles uneasily at her. "Sometimes you are truly a mystery to me, Marie."

She says nothing. She looks pleased by what he's said.

Miles could not find Lorraine, although he called to her repeatedly from the bedroom. "Lorraine? Where are you, Lorraine?" He spent many minutes calling to her in that small house, but she did not answer, and at last he resigned himself to the awful idea that she was outside, that she had left the house.

He went to the front door, reached, turned the knob. It wasn't locked. He let go of the knob, backed away from the door.

He would put some clothes on before going outside, he decided. He was naked, vulnerable, exposed. He clutched at himself and went back to his bedroom.

He closed the curtains and the room grew darker. He liked the darkness. He lay on his back on the bed, the blankets pulled up to his neck.

After a few moments, he rolled to his side and drew his knees up tightly to his chest.

He wept, but stopped before long, then listened to the sounds of the forest—wind, birdsong, the occasional noises of small animals moving about on the forest floor.

Soon, he was asleep.

Lorraine couldn't find him. She called to him repeatedly: "Miles? Where are you, Miles?" But she got no response.

So, she resigned herself to the idea that he had come downstairs, without alerting her, and had left the house.

But she didn't want to leave the house to find him. That was the last thing she wanted to do. She didn't even want to look out the windows and was thankful that all of the drapes were closed.

He would come back to her. She had no doubt of it. He'd have to come back. He couldn't survive beyond the house, in the forest. Naked and alone.

She went to the front door, looked at it for a long time, then backed away from it, toward the stairs, which were close by. Her heel hit the lowest step. She glanced back, reached, grabbed the newel post, steadied herself.

She looked at the door again.

Is it locked? she wondered. *What if it's not locked?* she wondered. *What could get in here? What lives out there?*

She ran to the door, threw the bolt, locked the knob.

And the back door? she wondered.

She ran to it, noticed, as she moved through the kitchen, that there was no drape on it, saw bright white light beyond, lowered her head so she wouldn't have to look, so she wouldn't have to see what was in the light.

She tried the knob on the back door. It was locked.

She ran to the living room, hesitated, called "Miles?" again, tremblingly, and then went back to the bedroom.

The curtain was closed.

Closed? she wondered, then, in her fear and panic, forgot the thought.

There was a walk-in closet. She went into it, closed the door. It was very dark inside. She welcomed the dark.

TWENTY-FIVE

his is what C.J. remembered.

Everything.

He remembered the white bathroom door, the paint chipped here and there, the black paint beneath.

And he remembered the gleaming white sink and its water-spotted, stainless steel legs, the oak medicine cabinet, the cracked mirror, the shower curtain, the missing curtain rings, the modern bathtub, the flower ring decals, the overhead light and frosted globe.

He remembered the rasping noise from the other side of the white door.

He remembered the door opening fast and hard, as if some powerful and angry animal had thrown it open.

The moonlit dark. The wind.

And he remembered the people—heavy-boned, strongly muscled, broad, round heads, high cheekbones, short, wide noses. The people moving about in the moonlit dark, in the woods, in the wind, their naked bodies reflecting the creamy moonlight, so they looked like ghosts.

He remembered everything.

The room he was in was warm and stark and too bright. He yelled, "Turn the light off!" But no one responded.

He yelled again, "Turn the light off!"

No one responded.

He was strapped to the bed. He didn't know why. He wondered what he could possibly have done that would call for him to be strapped down, unable to move, able only to speak. "Turn the light off!" he yelled again, and added, "Dammit!"

The light stayed on.

He didn't recognize the room he was in. Its walls were bare and white, like the ceiling. The room was lit by a single bright bulb hanging from the ceiling in a black wire cage. The cage cast long, diagonal shadows in the room.

The floor was gray linoleum. There were flecks of red in it. These flecks were irregular in size and shape and C.J. thought they looked like flecks of blood. They moved if he looked at them long enough. They squirmed and changed shape, grew and shrank. C.J. thought that this was very startling. It terrified him, and he wished it would stop. "Stop!" he screamed.

It stopped.

The door, which was closed, had a small window in it with wire mesh running through it.

There was a tall, narrow window in the wall beside the bed. C.J. could just see this window if he craned his head back far enough that his neck hurt.

The straps holding him at the ankles and wrists were made of brown leather that was cracked and faded from use and age.

The blanket covering him was gray. It bore the name "Mercy" twice, in blue, at its bottom edges. C.J. couldn't see this, but he knew it was there, nonetheless.

"Turn the heat off," he yelled, "I'm boiling!" But the heat stayed on. There was a small grating in a corner of the ceiling, and that was where the heat came from, he supposed. It was a stupid place for heat to come from, though—didn't everyone know that heat *rose? Cold* air settled. The heat run should have been on the floor.

It was on the floor—not on the ceiling—he saw now. He'd been mistaken. It was in a far corner, to the left of the door. Heat rose from it. He could tell that heat rose from it because the wall above it shimmered from the turbulent air. He had noticed the same thing above his father's car hood on hot days. The turbulent air caused the light to bend, so everything above shimmered and shimmied.

There was no grating in the ceiling. That would have been stupid. He knew better than to put a grating in the ceiling.

He didn't like the diagonal shadows. They crisscrossed the room like webs and made him think of huge, dark spiders.

He didn't like the wire mesh in the window in the door, either. Windows shouldn't have wire mesh in them. It was ugly.

And he didn't like the red speckles in the linoleum, or having to crane his head until his neck hurt so he could see the long, narrow window near his bed. And he didn't like the fact that, when he looked out the window, there was nothing to see outside but a glaze of incandescent light from the bulb in the center of the ceiling.

He screamed, "Turn the light off! It's too bright!"

The light went off. Came on again. Went off. On. It flickered in spasms, grew as bright as any light he had ever seen, so bright that he had to close his eyes. Then it dimmed to single candlepower, brightened again, dimmed, flashed, dimmed, brightened. The strobe-effect made him dizzy, and made his head ache.

Then, at last, the light was dead and the room was very,

very dark. There were no outlines to see. No light from beyond the door, through the window and its wire mesh. No light from the window near the bed.

And he knew where he was.

He rose.

He did not dare walk. His eyes needed to adjust to the darkness, first.

He would wait.

He had no choice.

"What do you think?" the orderly asked the nurse attending to C.J. The nurse was taking C.J.'s pulse. It was slow, and his skin was unusually cool, and pale. It was almost translucent. She thought that she could see the intricate patterns of the veins and capillaries. She thought she could almost see the hard grin of the bone beneath the skin. His eyes were open wide, fixed and staring, pupils dilated.

The nurse glanced at the orderly and said, "I think we should get the doctor in here, stat!"

TWENTY-SIX

Miles woke. The room was bathed in light.

He turned his head and glanced at the digital clock radio on the table near the bed. It wasn't working. He rolled over, grabbed the radio's AC cord, pulled gently on it. It resisted. It was plugged in.

He touched the button that turned the radio on. Nothing.

The light in the room was red, dazzling. It touched everything and changed its color to red—the white bookcase, the brown upholstered rocker, the dark cherry dresser, the gray digital clock radio. Everything was red.

A sunset, he thought.

The curtains over the window were red; they filtered the light into the room.

He rose. He said to himself, *I'm not remembering something. I should be remembering something, but I'm not.*

He thought that Lorraine should be in the room. Hadn't she been here when he went to sleep? Maybe she'd gone to school. Unfinished work, deadline work.

Lorraine? he wondered. "Girlfriend," he whispered.

He crossed to the window, drew the curtains.

The sun was red, huge and brilliant through the trees. It was falling swiftly toward the horizon, taking daylight with it. He watched it fall and thought, *This is what I didn't remember. Being here! In this place!*

Something touched him softly from behind. A hand, warm and small. It was a familiar touch, a caress. Lorraine's hand.

He turned his head, relieved that she was there with him. He wanted to smile, wanted to say something loving to her, but the smile and the words wouldn't come.

She wasn't there. The room had changed to rust-red and it was empty. But her touch persisted. It moved up his back to his shoulder, then down, to his buttocks. Her fingers pushed gently, rippling his skin.

A chill ran through him.

Her touch dissipated.

He turned, faced the room. Rust-red had become brown. All the furnishings were brown.

And a figure stood quietly in the doorway, its broad, round head cocked, dark eyes intent on him.

Miles stared back. The figure in the doorway was nearly the color of the light in the room. Its arms hung loosely at its sides. It stood erect, powerful-looking.

Miles whispered, "Who are you?"

The light in the room grew dimmer and the figure in the doorway continued to stare at him. Miles could not see its eyes now, only dark ovals.

The thing screamed deep within its chest, a moist, ear-splitting, horrific scream, low and demanding, full of anger and confusion. And very threatening.

Miles backed away as if the air itself, heavy with the weight of the scream, had pushed him back.

And when he stopped, the thing in the doorway was still screaming. The scream was everywhere. It was a part of the darkness itself.

Miles put his hands to his ears and ran to the walk-in closet. Its door was open; he threw himself inside and slammed the door shut behind him.

The screamer followed. Miles could hear him at the other side of the door.

Miles backed far into the black closet, felt his naked body hit the wall, heard, through his hands, still covering his ears, the screamer beyond the door.

All at once, he heard nothing.

Then the sound of feet moving down the stairway that led to the first floor.

WHAT HAPPENED THE DAY AARON GOT LOST

"I heard that hissing noise the day that Mommy got murdered. It was in the morning, before I got up. I was lying in my bed, tired. I had been dreaming and I was awake, and I was trying to remember the dream. It's funny that I remember most everything, but I can't remember my dreams.

"And I heard the hissing noise in the house. Not so much in my room, but in the house. Like it was in the walls, like a snake had gotten stuck in the walls. A hundred snakes. Millions of snakes stuck in the walls of the house.

"It was so loud and it was so much *everywhere* that I thought it was a strange kind of wind. A wind whooshing through cracks in the house, maybe.

"But I didn't think it was a wind. And I still don't think so. It wasn't a wind. I have never heard a wind like it if it was a wind.

"But I heard it the morning that Mommy got murdered

by a woman who came to visit her in the kitchen before
Daddy and I got up and went downstairs.

"I heard a strange wind and I wanted to call to my dad
about it but I didn't think he'd hear me, the wind was so
loud.

"I laid in bed and listened to the wind.

"Then it stopped.

"And I heard people talking downstairs. My mom.
Someone else. A woman. I didn't know who it was, then.

"That's when I got out of bed and went downstairs and
found Mommy.

"She had red marks on her throat. Her eyes were open
and her tongue was sticking out. Daddy said she had been
strangled by someone very, very strong. Because they broke
her neck, too. I could see that they broke her neck. It was
bent backwards. A little bit of blood was on her throat,
where her skin had cracked. But the blood did not flow,
because she was dead, and I know about such things because I read about them.

"I read quite a lot.

"I know many, many things.

"The capital of Kansas: Topeka. The height of the CN
Tower: 1,726 feet. It's the tallest free-standing structure in
the world. The population of Buffalo, New York: 1.3 million in 1981.

"I know that black holes are collapsed stars and that a
piece of a black hole the size of a thimble would weigh one
million tons. This seems like a silly thing to estimate and it
does not seem to me that anyone can ever prove such a
thing.

"And I know that human life came out of Africa, four
million years ago, and that it spread all over the earth from
there.

"I know that the substance which gives skin its color is called 'melanin.'

"I know that hair and fingernails do not grow after a body is dead, as many people believe. I know that it appears to grow because the skin shrinks.

"My mom's hair was dark, and long. And her skin was olive-colored. She was very pretty. She spoke in a soft voice that made everyone listen, because she never spoke unless there was something important to say. Daddy used to say that. He would talk about my mom, after she was dead, and that was one of the things he would say. He would also say that she was a 'wonderful, wonderful person.' Then he would start to cry and he couldn't say any more.

"I know also about photosynthesis, DNA, genetic engineering, red shift, lines of latitude and longitude.

"I know who killed my mother. I know who did it, now. Marie did it.

"My head aches sometimes and I want to make it blank, so that there is no information in it. Sometimes I want to be like a door or a chair or a window. Something inanimate. Then all this information in my head wouldn't be! I would have no head. I would have no life.

"I know about archaeology. And about anthropology.

"I know about book binding. Perfect binding. Letterpress printing. Offset printing.

"I know what 'whorls' are.

"I know that the things that make everything up never change. And time, Dad says, is only a measurement of change. If there is really no change there is really no time. We see things change and we say, Look, that has changed. It was that way before, and now it is this way, so the thing that occurred between *then* and *now* is called 'time.' But it cannot be, because nothing really changes. The tiny particles that make up everything do not change. The atoms and the quarks and the electrons. They do not change.

"I don't know what Daddy's talking about when he says things like that. It confuses me. Sometimes I think it confuses him, too, and he's merely talking about it so he can try to make sense of it. But I don't want to tell him this because he likes to talk about such things, and he thinks I understand. But I don't. Not always.

"My mom was buried. She was dead, then, when she was buried. But she was alive, too. In my memory. The mom who was buried is not the mom who is alive in my memory. The mom in my memory talks to me. She has many, many things to say and she says them over and over again, because I never get tired of hearing the things that she says. That mom, the one in my memory, is not the mom who was laying on the floor, and that mom is not the one in the ground. They're all different moms. My mom didn't change from being alive to being dead. My mom is in my head and she talks to me, she says things to me over and over again, and as long as I'm alive, then so is she."

TWENTY-SEVEN

Miles stayed in the dark walk-in closet in his bedroom for a very long time. Often, he heard the closet door being handled, touched, prodded. The doorknob, too. There was no lock on the door. Anyone wanting to get in needed only to turn the knob. But it wasn't turned. It was touched. And prodded. As if the hands touching were not used to turning doorknobs.

He heard people walking about softly in the room beyond. Two people, he guessed, maybe three. Occasionally, he heard what could have been speech, but the words were unintelligible, spoken in low, guttural tones that were also oddly musical.

Miles progressed beyond fear while he sat in the dark in the closet. He became separated from himself, aware of his body in the closet, aware of his wide and staring eyes, his sweat, the hot, moist air, the clothes that hung neatly from wooden hangers—his shirts and suits and sports jackets.

He watched himself from outside himself.

But, after a while, the sounds of people moving about beyond the door dissipated and the dark in the closet became comforting and reassuring, though only for the moment. He had begun to live for the moment—that moment when blessed silence ruled the house, the moment that evolved into several moments of blessed silence.

After a long while, he climbed back into himself.

He became aware of his nakedness. No one could see him there, in the closet, but his nakedness still made him feel vulnerable, was still a condition that was uncivilized and uncontemporary (the thing in the doorway had appeared to be naked).

So, after what seemed like many hours after he had put himself in the closet, he stood and groped on the hangers for some clothes to wear. He found a sports jacket; he could tell it was a sports jacket because of its weave—heavy, utilitarian wool—his rust-colored, herringbone tweed sports jacket, he guessed. Then he found a pair of pants. They were soft, his gray dress pants, he supposed, which went best with his blue blazer. He groped in the dark for the blazer but couldn't find it. He remembered. It was at the cleaners. He'd spilled cranberry juice cocktail on it at a formal reception in his honor three weeks earlier.

He dressed in the heavy wool sports jacket and soft pants, then got down on his hands and knees and groped for shoes. He had several pairs—black wing tips, which he never wore, a pair of scuffed and time-worn Hush Puppies that were very comfortable, a pair of Wallabees that he had just purchased and which were still in their box, several pairs of sneakers—Nike, Adidas, and Reeboks. The Nikes were ankle height, the Adidas and Reeboks were tennis shoes. He found the black wing tips, could feel the swirling pattern of holes in the toe and around the sides. He grimaced. Surely the Hush Puppies were close by. He was reasonably neat about his clothes and shoes; he didn't simply leave them where he took them off. He usually put them here, in this closet, in a line with his other shoes. But he could find only the wing tips. He didn't even know if they fit.

He tried them on. He had no socks here, in the closet, and the shoes, never having been worn, were hard and uncomfortable; one of them had a small crease in the inner lining, near his instep, and it pushed into his foot when he stood. Eventually, it would wear the skin away, he realized, so he took the shoe off and tore out the lining, exposing the soft, cottony substance beneath.

He felt relieved. He'd solved the problem of the uncomfortable wing tips. It was a tiny victory, but it made him smile.

And, smiling, he opened the closet door and stepped out into the bedroom.

It was night. He stopped smiling.

He could see well enough. Moonlight filtered through the window.

The curtains had been pulled from it.

The blankets had been ripped from the bed.

The dresser drawers had been scattered about.

The bedroom was a mess.

Where, he wondered, had *he* been while all this was going on? He'd been in the closet, only a couple of yards away. But he had heard next to nothing. He had heard people moving quietly about, heard the doorknob being touched.

Why hadn't he been aware of this mayhem going on?

He made his way across the room to the light switch near the door and flicked it on. The overhead light came on, startling him. He hadn't expected the light to work.

It went off.

He flicked the switch off, then on again. The light came on. Off. On. It stayed on.

Substandard wiring, he thought.

He crossed to the bed. The digital clock radio was working. It read 3:23 A.M. He turned the radio on. *American Pie* blared out; it was near the end of the song—"Bye, bye, Miss American Pie, drove my Chevy to the levee but the levee was dry—" He turned it off.

This couldn't be.

He went to the window, looked out, saw only his own reflection from the glass. "Damn!" he whispered, and crossed the room to the wall switch, flicked it off, went back to the window.

He saw creamy moonlight on rolling, grass-covered hills. No trees. No houses.

He looked more closely, put his face to the window. There were irregularly spaced rectangular holes in the earth. Neat piles of lumber. A narrow road.

He straightened. "Good Lord!" he breathed. He'd come back. But he hadn't come back all the way. This scenario—the rectangular holes in the earth, the narrow road, the piles of lumber—was what?—something from ten years ago, five?

He heard a wind start.

He looked out the window again, straining to see. He thought that the grasses on the rolling hills were motionless, although it is nearly impossible to tell in moonlight whether trees or grasses are moving. The eye settles on stillness, likes it, finds it easy to deal with and interpret.

But the grasses weren't moving. He was certain of it.

The wind grew in strength and volume. The windowpane rattled and whined.

He straightened, glanced at the digital clock radio. Its glowing, soft blue numerals read 3:27 A.M. As he watched, the numerals went to black, then came back on again almost at once; 3:27. They went out again, came back on, flashed *12:00,* went out.

The wind screamed. He remembered the scream of the creature in the doorway. This scream was similar. It was strong and insistent and threatening.

He looked out the window again.

He saw trees close by the house. Branches reaching for the window. An inverted, pie-shaped slice of moonlit sky.

He gasped and stumbled backwards toward the bed in his wing tips and herringbone tweed jacket and soft gray pants. He hit the bed, sat down hard on it, bent forward, put his face in his hands.

His hands felt very cool; the jacket smelled of aftershave. The mattress lay askew on the box spring and he knew that he was sitting on it as it perched partially over open air and that he was lucky he hadn't simply pitched onto the floor when he sat down.

He realized that he was beyond fear, awe, astonishment.

The earth had changed.

Time had changed.

But *he* had not changed.

He was whole, intact, complete. That was important; he could take some comfort from it. His blood flowed, his heart beat, and his brain registered his environment—mattress perched over open air, his cool hands, the tang of aftershave on his sports jacket.

Everything else—the rest of the universe—had turned upside down and inside out, but *he* was exactly as he should be. Whole, complete, and intact. Ten fingers and ten toes.

Would he *know* if he had changed? he wondered.

Of course he would. He was Miles Gale, archaeologist, thirty-eight years old. He had two sons. Aaron and C.J. And he had had two wives. Joanna and Marie.

Joanna was dead.

Marie was missing.

Aaron was missing, too.

He had been missing for quite a few days, two weeks or more.

And there was someone named Lorraine. Tall, red-haired. Very attractive. Who was she? How well did he know her? He thought it was possible that he knew her very well.

Lorraine *what?* He should know her last name. He could see her face in his mind's eye, could feel her touch, hear her voice. He should know her *name,* for Christ's sake!

Parts were missing from his memory and from his life. But why? Because here, in the past, what had created those memories—the people and the places and the events—were far in the future? Wasn't that a respected tenet of all time-travel stories? Of course, because it made sense, and he was a sensible man.

Would he forget *everything?* His own name, his sons' names, his occupation, the names of his brothers and sisters, where he had lived as a child, how many pets he had owned, et cetera, et cetera?

Or maybe he was losing his memory because it was nature's way of getting him ready for his new life. His rebirth. Here. In the distant past.

Was it the past? How could he be sure? What proof did he have but intuition?

He patted his sports coat pocket. It was usually littered with pencils and pens, and he hoped to find one now. He found the stub of a pencil in his inside pocket, felt for a piece of paper, and located one quickly enough—a receipt from a 7-Eleven.

He went to the end table near the bed, and wrote, in very small letters, on the back of the receipt:

Lorraine. Marie. Joanna. Aaron. He stopped. There was someone else. Who?

"Fuck!" he whispered. He couldn't remember his other son's name.

C.L., he scribbled. He smiled. He was pleased by remembering. He looked at the initials. *C.L.?* he wondered. No. It wasn't "C.L." It was "C.J." He crossed out *C.L.* and wrote *C.J.* Good. His memory was complete. He was whole. Intact. He would survive here.

He folded the piece of paper and put it into the right breast pocket of his jacket.

TWENTY-EIGHT

A jet contrail was the only blemish on the clear mid-November morning sky.

"Problem?" Lorraine heard.

She lowered her gaze. One of the neighbors—a stout, unhealthy-looking man named Peter Harvey—was looking at her. He had lugged a bulging black plastic garbage bag to the curb and was still holding onto its yellow drawstring.

Lorraine stared at him a moment. She was on Miles's front porch.

Peter Harvey called, "Is something wrong, Miss Rabkin?"

Neighbors, she thought. There was nothing judgmental in the thought. This man was simply one of Miles's neighbors. Miles had plenty of neighbors, none of them very friendly.

She called, her voice trembling, "Have you seen Miles?"

Peter Harvey, eyes red and bulbous from too much alcohol, looked blankly at her, as if he hadn't understood her question, and said, "No. Lost him, have you?"

"I'm not sure . . . where he is," she said.

Peter Harvey continued staring at her for a few seconds, then checked his watch, looked back at Lorraine, turned, and went silently up his driveway to his house.

* * *

These, C.J. realized, were the drumlins that would some-day, far in the future, be leveled to make way for the Trip-hammer Mall. They were grass-covered and dotted with birch saplings—thin, and white, and spiky. Tall saw grass and birch saplings covered quite a wide area around the drumlins, in fact. The aftermath of a forest fire—quick, and incredibly destructive, but somehow contained to the sev-eral hundred acres that C.J. was looking at. Perhaps there was a natural firebreak at the perimeter of the grassy area. Perhaps the fire had been put out by rainstorms.

C.J. had learned about the aftermath of forest fires from his reading. It was one of the millions of bits of information his memory made available to him.

The sky was heavy with bulging, dark, cumulous clouds—the sun was only a light swatch of gray near the horizon, and the air was still, moist and hard to breathe; it carried the tang of pine, and, faintly, the sickly sweet and biting odor of skunk.

C.J. stood at the brow of a high hill that overlooked the grass and sapling-covered drumlins and the forests a mile or more beyond. He had just emerged from a stand of woods.

Not far in front of him, down the slope, something lum-bered through the tall grass, which swayed and straight-ened, swayed and straightened. C.J. thought that it was a gopher, a muskrat or a beaver on its way to the lake three quarters of a mile to his left, down the steep slope.

He was unaccustomed to wild creatures in such close proximity to himself, although his reading had told him that muskrats, beavers, and gophers would not attack a human being, and he backed away.

The creature moving through the grass went farther down the slope and he could not see the grass swaying anymore. This relieved him. "Good," he whispered, and the sound of his voice in the still, heavy air startled him.

He waited a few seconds and started down the slope himself, in the general direction that the creature had gone—toward the lake.

It drew him. It was familiar, apparently unchanged; its contours, from this vantage point, were exactly as he remembered. There was the little peninsula jutting from the lake's western edge. In the future, C.J. knew, boats would dock there. And, on the lake's east side—the side he was walking toward—was the small cove . . . He stopped walking, looked closer. No cove. The beginnings of a cove, perhaps. A little crescent-shaped spit of bare land. But the cove had yet to form. It was still hidden beneath the lake's waters, which, over time, would recede.

But he could see the island, and it made him smile. Frontenac Island, the site of his father's most recent digs. Six to twenty-three inches deep in refuse middens—garbage cast off by the area's Archaic inhabitants, the Laurentian people, whom his father had written and talked about so much. The people who had lived here six thousand years ago.

He started walking again, his eyes intent on the island, a swath of gray on the dark blue waters of the lake.

He stopped. He had seen movement on the island. Much movement, as if the island itself were alive.

WHAT HAPPENED THE DAY
AARON GOT LOST

"I told Daddy, 'There's a woman in the cellar.'

"He was in the kitchen, having coffee and doughnuts. Sugar doughnuts. He used to eat lots of sugar doughnuts, then he stopped eating them. He stopped eating anything that had sugar. He thought he was getting a paunch, he said. And he was.

"Daddy said, 'A woman in the cellar?' He smiled. I could tell he thought I was making it up. But it was a funny smile, too, like he was wondering why I would make up something like that.

"I nodded at him and he asked me, 'What's she doing in the cellar?'

" 'Just standing there without any clothes on,' I said. 'I can't see her face or nothing,' I said, ''cuz she's looking at the wall, Dad, and it's dark down there, too.'

"And he stopped smiling and his eyebrows came together and he reached out and took my shoulders. He seems very, very big in my memory.

"He said, 'Why don't you go upstairs and play with your Matchbox cars, sport? I'll go down to the cellar, okay?'

"I went upstairs and played with my Matchbox cars. I played with them for a little while, until I got tired of them, then I went down to the cellar.

"I found my dad there.

"What he was doing was looking at the skull that he had brought home in its own dirt box. I could see him doing this from the cellar stairs, which I stopped halfway down on because I could see him there and I thought he'd get mad at me for not being in my room, where he had asked me to go.

"He was touching the skull in the box. He had his fingers on the top of it and was running them along the skull. I could see his back and the side of his face, and the skull, which was to his left on a worktable that was down in the cellar in that house.

"He did not see me, I think. He didn't turn to look at me. I was very quiet. I thought he looked strange touching that skull. I thought that the skull was very ugly and I thought that my dad was being strange touching it like that, because it was the way that he used to touch my mom, on her arm, or on her face, so his fingers just moved along her skin. It was nice to see him do that, to touch my mom. But I did not like him touching the skull in that same way. It was like he loved the skull and I didn't know why he would love the skull.

"It was nighttime and the cellar was dark, except for the fluorescent work light that is above the table where Dad did his work. I could see him and the skull and some of the table. Everything else around was dark.

"The woman I saw was in the dark and she was being very still and she was nearby to my dad, and she was reaching out for him. Then she wasn't there because I started to cry, and she went away, back into the dark. And my dad turned around and saw me, and came across the cellar very fast. I was crying, and he said, 'What's wrong, sport? Are you all right?' And my eyes were sort of closed, and I couldn't see very well through my crying, but I could see things, anyway, although they were very hazy, like I was looking through a rainy window, and when I looked at him, there was the woman behind him, and she had her arms out to him and she was moving at him from behind, with her arms out, not walking, or running, but moving behind him. And then my dad came up the stairs. And she came up the stairs, not moving her legs, but coming up the stairs after him like she was floating, and I saw her eyes, but not her face very much, and her eyes were yellow, their color was yellow. And they stared at my dad like she was some sort of animal, some sort of cat or something, and my dad was what she was after.

"Then my dad picked me up and she went away.

"And it was five months later that Lorraine brought her over and her name was Marie, and she married my dad and had Aaron, my little brother."

TWENTY-NINE

C. J. ran hard, up the slope, toward the stand of woods he had just come out of; he cast quick and fearful glances behind him at Frontenac Island as he ran.

He went a dozen yards into the stand of woods, and stopped, turned around, looked back. The island was nearly a mile away, down the steep slope. It was small, dark gray, slipper-shaped, and it hugged close to the tree-lined northern shore of the lake. The lake water around it—especially at its northern edge, which was close to the shore—was almost white; the water there was shallow enough to walk in, C.J. knew. The rest of the narrow lake was dark blue, signifying its depth—because of the heavy overcast, that dark blue was nearly black—and, due to the stillness of the air, the water was flat and motionless.

C.J. looked breathlessly at the island for a long while.

He could see little vegetation on it, only a spindly and stunted pine at the tip of its southern edge. The rest of the island was covered with dark gray refuse middens and what could have been small log shelters; from C.J.'s vantage point, it was hard to tell.

But it was the island's *movement* that transfixed him and frightened him. It was as if the island's skin were crawling.

The sun poked briefly through the heavy overcast, and

C.J. saw moving points of dull light on the island, as if it were iridescent. The image that came to him was of a huge dead fish covered with bluebottle flies. But these moving points of light were dull red, vaguely worm-shaped, and they were everywhere.

Then the sun was gone, the moving points of light disappeared, and he was seeing only the island's dark gray skin crawling again.

He wanted to get closer. He desperately *needed* to get closer, to find out exactly what he was seeing. Because islands didn't have skins, and islands didn't move.

Especially Frontenac Island, which was a place of death, a place he had visited with his father more than once, a place that fascinated him and repulsed him, and terrified him. Just as it was doing now.

He moved a couple of steps forward, to the perimeter of the stand of woods.

He could move no closer to the island. His fear fought his compulsion and made him motionless.

"Dammit!" he screamed.

Moments later, the island stilled.

"Hell," the doctor muttered, "when is this heat going to be fixed? It's like an oven in here!"

An orderly standing behind him said, "Want I should shut the heat grate off, Doc?"

The doctor glanced quickly at him, shook his head, and looked at a nurse standing nearby. The nurse was looking expectantly at him and seemed very confused. The doctor said, "I want some more blankets in here."

"Blankets?" said the nurse. "But, Doctor, it's so hot—"

"This child is freezing. We've got to raise his body temperature. Now please get some more blankets."

The nurse nodded briskly, then said to the orderly, "You know where the storage room is?" It was the orderly's first day.

"Yes," he said, and left the room; the storage area was seconds away. He would be gone for less than half a minute.

Another doctor came into the room as the orderly left, hurried over to the bed, and gasped. "His skin," the doctor said, "it's *translucent.*"

The first doctor glanced at her. "The condition seems progressive. I have no idea what's causing it. Respiration is normal; we're getting a blood count. His body temperature is way low, however, incredibly low—"

"Jesus," the second doctor cut in, "you can see the *bone—*"

Miles thought that the simple act of opening his front door had been the hardest thing he had ever done. Harder than the time so long ago (How old had he been? Twelve? Fifteen?) that he had had to take his beloved cocker spaniel (yellow Lab? Irish setter?) to the veterinarian to be "put down," as his mother had called it. Harder even than being point man the few times he had seen combat in Vietnam. Harder than telling his youngest (oldest?) son that . . . Marie, his second wife (first wife?), the boy's mother (What *was* her name—Marie? Joanne? Roxanne?) was missing.

But the front door was open now. It stood open and it revealed the dense forest that crowded the house. The forest was still and quiet in the hot, humid air.

Miles, standing just inside the house, had his mouth open in awe. A fast-moving insect buzzed in from the forest and circled near his face. Miles closed his mouth and lashed out at the insect, which flew farther into the house.

He stepped forward, so the top of the doorway was above him.

He could see no underbrush or grasses, only trees. Pines predominated. A lone and towering red oak—its trunk massive, gray and gnarled by age—stood close by.

Here and there, an irregular patch of the sullen and overcast sky was visible.

From very deep within the forest, Miles heard birdsong. It was brief, high-pitched; young birds, he thought. Birds in the nest.

He put his hands to the doorjamb and leaned forward, out the door, keeping his feet on the sill. He looked to his right. Trees. He looked to his left. Trees.

He pulled himself back to a standing position under the door, but kept his hands on the doorjamb.

This thought came to him: *Is this* my *house?* He noted the thought, and, as quickly as it came to him, it was gone, and he ignored it.

He glanced back, into the house's interior. Briefly, it was strange to him. He didn't recognize the furnishings—the Queen Anne couch, the overstuffed chair, the brass wall lamp. None of it was familiar to him. And then it was. Foyer. Kitchen to the left. Downstairs bathroom at the back, beyond the living room. His study to the right of the bathroom. The stairs.

He turned his head so his gaze was on the forest again, and thought, *This is a very unusual place for me to have put my house.*

He cocked his head. From deep within the forest, he heard birdsong. It pleased him. He smiled. *Young birds,* he thought. *Birds in the nest.*

A drop of rain stained the thick, dry mat of pine needles that was the forest floor. Miles stepped out the door, into the forest. He looked up. A roughly circular patch of gray sky was visible above the house. The rain would come through there.

He went back into the house and closed the door gently behind him.

"Josh?" he called.

Where was Josh? It was his turn to set the table.

Josh? *Josh?* What was he thinking? Josh was his older brother and he'd been dead for ten years. Why was he calling to him to come and set the table—that was a chore they had done when they were kids. They weren't kids, anymore. Josh wasn't *any*thing anymore, and he—Miles—was thirty-eight years old, and he had a family, two boys (three boys?), and a wife, Joanna (Jo) and a career, and . . .

Is this my house? Miles wondered.

He didn't know.

This is *my house!* he told himself.

But whose house was it really, and why had it been built in the middle of a forest?

"Lorraine!" he called. "Where are you? I need you!"

Was she at work? Doing some last-minute research? Why hadn't she told him where she was going? Why had she left without saying anything?

"Lorraine?" he called.

Maybe she was upstairs.

Upstairs? Did this house *have* an upstairs? He glanced about. Living room, a closed door beyond—it led to a bedroom, no doubt.

Bathroom door open. Kitchen to his left. No stairway. No upstairs. He should have known that! The house was a one-story house. Of course it was a one-story house. It had always *been* a one-story house. He had once lived in a two-story house that was nearly identical to this one; he could see it in his mind's eye. He cocked his head. It *was* identical, except that it had two stories, and this house had only one. And he was seeing it indistinctly, as if through a haze, as if he were recalling a dream.

From above, he heard the faint patter of rain, and he remembered the break in the trees. The rain was coming through it. He liked the sound of rain. It was comforting. This house was well situated. It allowed the rain to fall on it. All houses should be built where rain could reach them.

"Marie?" he called. *Marie?* he wondered. Was he still married to Marie? He remembered her. He could see her in his mind's eye in much the way that he could see that other house, as if she were looking at him through a haze, as if he were recalling a vivid dream.

He went into the kitchen and rummaged about in the cupboards. It was midday. Time for lunch.

But the cupboards were empty. No food, no plates, glasses, odds and ends. Of course. It was a brand-new house. He'd just moved in. He and Josh, and Marie. Jo. Aaron. He and his little family had just moved in. And Marie (Jo?) was out stocking up on food. Buying food. (Collecting food? Gathering food?)

"C.L.?" he called.

C.L.? Was it C.L.? Wasn't it something else? C.W.? C.J.? C.N.?

C.N.? he wondered.

C.N. Tower.

Canada. Canadian.

Canadian National Exhibition. Royal Canadian Mounted Police. Royal pain in the ass. Ass . . . ask me no questions, I'll tell you no lies, lies like a rug, toupee, Ferde Grofé, Grand Canyon Suite, Oh my sweet, my sweet! Sweets to the sweet, suite of furniture, $39.00 a month, a monk, the

monk, the monk, the Monkees, Montereys, Monterey Jack,
Jack shit, eat shit and die, die, die my darling, my darling,
my sweet, my sweet . . .

Miles clasped his hands hard over his ears and screamed.

Lorraine had just come back inside from talking to Peter
Harvey and she glanced up the stairs and wondered what
she had heard. A brief moan? A whisper? The quick chirp
of an insect?

"Miles?" she called from the bottom of the stairs. There
was no reply.

"Miles?"

She started up the stairs, slowly at first, then more
quickly. She got to the landing, hesitated, and went to each
of the four bedrooms on the second floor of the house and
looked quickly into each one.

Then she went back downstairs.

People, C.J. realized. He should have known. He thought
that he *had* known, but the memory had just . . . slipped by.
There were *people* all over that island, *people* making it look
like it was alive. *People!*

The Laurentian people. ·

The same people his dad had written about and talked
about. The same people who had lived six thousand years
ago, and who had buried their dead beneath the refuse
middens on that island. Frontenac Island. *Frontenac?* The
name seemed unfamiliar. He thought. Remembered. Yes.
That's what it was called. Frontenac Island. He couldn't
possibly forget that.

He forgot nothing.

And now Frontenac Island was still because the people
on it, the people who covered it like skin, had heard him

yell, had stopped what they were doing, and were looking up at him from a mile away, down the steep slope.

Could they see him?

He stepped quickly to his left, so he was behind the sheltering trunk of a tall white pine.

Of course they couldn't see him. It was a long way from there to here. And it was raining. How could they see him?

The island moved again. It *slithered.*

Its south end, the end facing the bulk of the lake, became still; the shallow white water at the north end, so close to the tree-lined shore, grew dark with movement.

Frontenac Island was emptying itself of its people.

C.J. watched, dumbfounded, as the white water separating the island from the shore grew dark with people. Where were they going? he wondered. They couldn't possibly know he was here. It was such a long way. Even if they'd heard him yell, they couldn't have *seen* him at this distance. Even they—hundreds of them on the island and in the water—were, to his eyes, simply a moving, dark mass. He couldn't distinguish *individuals,* and his vision was excellent.

He glanced back, into the stand of woods.

He had no choice, he realized. He had to keep away from these people.

He turned, found the narrow path he had followed to get to the slope that overlooked Frontenac Island, and took it back into the stand of woods.

Lorraine was confused and very frightened. So frightened, in fact, that she was sweating, and her breathing was labored. It was the fear and confusion caused by not knowing, the kind of claustrophobic and numbing fear that waking from a nightmare into another nightmare creates.

From across the street, Peter Harvey called, "Still haven't found him?"

She stared at the man from the front doorway of Miles's house. She shook her head stiffly.

Peter Harvey called, "Maybe he's at work."

She shook her head again.

"You okay?" Peter Harvey called.

She looked silently at the man for a moment, then stepped back into the house and closed the door.

Miles was in the house!

Miles was not *in the house!*

He was accessible, inaccessible. Alive. Lost. Hiding.

"Goddammit, Miles, where *are* you?" she yelled.

The house stayed quiet.

She listened. She heard the furnace turn on below, in the basement.

She glanced about, at the foyer, the living room—the Queen Anne couch, the overstuffed chair, the brass wall lamp—the hallway that led to the kitchen.

There were doors closed here, she realized. One in the foyer, one in the living room.

The closed doors were closet doors.

For God's sake, she hadn't looked in the *closets!*

THIRTY

Refuse middens, C.J. thought, sounded like something you put on your hands so you could take out the garbage. He grinned at the thought. *C.J., put on your refuse middens, it's Monday evening.*

Again?

Don't complain. We all have chores to do around here. No one is immune.

A blackfly bit him on the cheek. He swatted at it and hit himself on the cheek, hard. "Dammit!" he whispered.

He saw that there were blackflies everywhere. They flew erratically, soundlessly. There were several clusters of two or three that formed tight little flying knots. Occasional high-pitched buzzing noises came from these flying knots.

Another fly bit him, on the arm this time. He swatted, missed.

June, he thought. *Blackfly season.*

June? What was that? What was *June?*

The air was heavy and humid; it smelled of pine tar and damp tree bark. It was not an unpleasant mixture of smells, but the air was difficult to breathe, as if there were a wet washcloth stretched over his mouth and nose.

He thought, *June. The sixth month. June, July, August.*

He heard a quick noise behind him—someone coughing, someone saying "Hello," perhaps.

He turned around and peered hard into the stand of woods; it was darker, now, from the gathering dusk.

He saw the trees all around. There was no underbrush, only the still trees and the dark spaces between.

The rain had stopped. It had been raining in the clearing that overlooked Frontenac Island. But it was not raining here. He looked up. The foliage was too thick. It blocked the rain.

A bird flitted from one tree to another. The bird was small and red. He knew about birds, he knew the names of a thousand kinds of birds, but he couldn't place this one.

He lowered his head and saw nearby the flash of a broad brownish back and arm. "What . . ." he said. Then there was nothing, only the stillness, the dark spaces between the trees, the gathering dusk.

"Hello," he heard. But it was not "hello," he realized. It was something else. Something *like* "hello."

He thought frantically that the Frontenac Island people had found him, that they were all around him in the woods, and that he couldn't see them, but that they could see him, that they were watching him at that very moment, that there were a hundred pairs of eyes on him.

He was thankful for the quickly gathering dusk. It would hide him.

"Hello," he heard again. But it was closer to a monosyllable, now. An expression of surprise. Or pain.

He listened.

"Uh!" he heard, but he could not gauge where the sound had come from. It had been too quick; had seemed to come from everywhere.

The air began to cool. Individual trees, at the close horizon, became lost in darkness.

"Uh!" he heard. "Uh-nuh!"

He craned his head around, without turning his body, and looked toward the source of the sound. There was a space between two pines close by. A man stood in this space. He was short, heavily muscled, dark-skinned, naked. He supported himself with one hand against the trunk of one of the pines. His head was lowered.

"Uh-nuh!" he repeated. "Uh!"

C.J. shook his head to say he didn't understand what the man was saying.

The man fell face forward onto the forest floor; his legs buckled first, then his upper body pitched hard into the mat of pine needles, so he hit it with his forehead, arms flapping uselessly as he fell. He seemed to make no effort whatever to cushion himself, and C.J. knew at once that he was dead.

The orderly came in with the blankets. He hesitated, then, after a glance from the doctor, started across the room.

The other doctor, standing by, said, "It's as if the child is simply . . . vanishing."

"That's very fanciful," said the first doctor scornfully, and reached out to take a blanket from the orderly.

Miles saw an apparition in his house. It was the apparition of a woman, and he did not recognize her. She moved frantically, as if looking for someone, and she was visible for mere moments at a time, as if she were crossing quickly in front of a doorway.

She was transparent, as apparitions often are, and she seemed to be calling to someone repeatedly, although Miles could not hear her words. He saw her lips move, saw her head turn, her eyes widen. And then she was gone.

Once, he reached for her, because she seemed to be nearly within arm's reach, but she turned away.

She didn't frighten him. He found her presence oddly comforting and reassuring, as if she were a piece of music he hadn't heard since childhood, and did not remember note for note, but which had soothed him then, and soothed him now.

He thought that she was very lovely.

He wanted to be able to touch her and talk to her, because he felt, oddly, that *he* was the one she was calling to, although he could not imagine why. He lived alone in his house.

He had always lived alone.

Four Years Earlier

Marie says, at the open window, "This is nothing. This is a weak child. A whisper. It's *bullshit!*" She turns and looks at C.J. She knows he's behind her in the doorway because she can see his reflection in the window. It's night; there's a storm, and a vicious wind is blowing; it shakes the big, sturdy house they live in.

Marie's golden eyes are reflecting light from the hallway. She smiles as if in grim and pleasurable anticipation. "Hello, weak child," she says to C.J.

She goes on, "Weak child. Like this wind. This bullshit. This miserable wind. *I* have seen a wind. I have been a *part* of a wind you could not even *listen* to, let alone be a part of."

Then she turns her head back to the window, raises her

arms up over her head like she's giving a cheer at a basketball game, and—with a strange, and oddly frightening childlike enthusiasm—she yells "Bullshit!" over and over again.

When Lorraine looked into the big, walk-in closet in the bedroom she and Miles shared, she did not see him at first. The overhead bulb was off and he was huddled in a corner—hanging clothes obscured her view of him—and his skin had taken on the color of the dim light in the room.

Miles wondered if he had always had the company of the apparition in his house. He couldn't remember. He thought that there was much he *should* remember, although he couldn't imagine why. His existence here, in his little house in the forest, was certainly peaceful enough. Clearly, it had *always* been peaceful.

He sat in his armchair as these thoughts came to him. It was well past dusk and the inside of the house was dark. He saw only the outlines of the house's scant furnishings. It came to him that he could turn on the lights, and, indeed, he once reached to turn on the lamp near his chair, but then decided that there was no real *need* for light in the house, that it was better to move with the ebb and flow of natural light, from evening to dawn to dusk to evening. The heartbeat of the earth and sun. Why disturb the night forest with incandescence?

There were times when he saw the apparition pass by. Now, for instance. She was close to him, motionless. She looked confused, and he felt oddly sorry for her because of her confusion. She disturbed the air slightly and he could sense this disturbance.

She wore a perfume that was reminiscent of . . . something—he had no idea what, but its smell excited him for a moment, and then started a moment's longing within him.

He thought that she was unreachable, like someone on a movie screen whose image he enjoyed, but whose substance and reality would forever be beyond him.

WHAT HAPPENED THE DAY
AARON GOT LOST

"It was in the middle of the afternoon when I saw the woman in the house.

"I was in the house, a different house than the one we have now. And I was downstairs in the hallway, on my way to the kitchen for some lemonade and I saw a woman at the other end of the hallway. I saw her and then she was gone. I did not see her face. She was facing away from me, facing the wall. She was naked and she had her arms up high and her legs together. She had no hair. I could tell that she was a woman because she did not look like a man. Her skin was dark, but not very dark. And she was not tall. She was not even as tall as I am, I think. There was light on her and I could see her very well.

"Then, later, Aunt Lisa was visiting, and she said, 'They were the first created things, the first living creatures. They had no form, per se. They took whatever form was convenient, whatever form pleased them.'

"My father smiled, like a grin.

"'I'm talking about the beginning of time, Miles,' said Aunt Lisa. 'When time itself started. Time, you know, did not simply *begin*—it did not simply start at, say, second one, then second two, second three. When it started, it . . . I don't know, it *was,* it emerged whole. Complete. Everything. And . . . demon life started then, to travel time at its own urging, and for its own amusement—'

"Miles?" Lorraine whispered, because, for an instant, she could not believe that what she was seeing was him. She thought that she might be seeing only a shadow, or a trick of the eye.

She came forward slowly, still disbelieving, through the darkened closet. But when she reached and pulled the chain for the light overhead, and saw him huddled in the corner, she gasped, backed up a step and looked disbelievingly at him for a moment. "Miles!" she exclaimed, and rushed forward, bent over him, put her hand on his arm; he was very cold and his skin was nearly transparent; she thought that she could see the hard grin of the bone beneath.

He was naked. His legs were outstretched and his arms hung loosely at his sides. He stared wide-eyed, apparently at nothing.

"Miles," Lorraine said, "what are you doing?" She could think of nothing else to say. "What's *wrong* with you, Miles? What are you *doing?*"

He did not answer.

THIRTY-ONE

Marie saw the way a fly does. She saw a hundred images, each slightly askew from the next because of the curve of her eye. Her brain brought all these images together and made them into several images, and, in turn, interpreted the different perspectives these several images gave it, then merged these images into one stereoscopic image.

Her brain received and interpreted events in much the way that a motion picture camera does; frame by frame. But, whereas a camera records up to approximately forty frames per second, Marie's eyes and brain recorded and interpreted millions of times that number of frames per second—in effect, they broke noncontinuous reality up into its component parts so she could study it, at will, and manipulate it to her own advantage.

She existed both outside of time, and within it, like water around a wheel.

And she was only as human as she wished to be.

The night sounds were unfamiliar to C.J. He heard something amble by, close to him in the forest's near-total darkness—its feet made gentle squishing noises on the soft forest floor—and he had no idea what name to assign to it.

Clearly, it was some creature that was much smaller than a man, but the names he needed so he could categorize what he was hearing—raccoon, opossum, muskrat—flickered just beyond his recognition and he was left only with vague and unsatisfying mental images.

There were bats, owls, other night birds, toads, and they all had their own distinct sounds. But C.J. recognized none of these sounds, though he had heard them often enough on overnight field trips with his father. He had learned to be frightened of nothing that ambles about, or talks to itself in monosyllables, or flits through the darkness in search of food in a forest at night. And he wasn't particularly frightened now. He had put what he thought was much distance between himself and the short, muscular man who had pitched forward, dead, onto the forest floor. He had found what he supposed would be good shelter; a broad-leafed deciduous tree bent over to the ground by a fallen white pine, so the deciduous tree formed a leafy dome which hid him well and sheltered him from the rain that had stopped only minutes ago.

There was no rain now. There was darkness (interrupted only by irregularly shaped swatches of dark gray sky, breaks in the canopy formed by the trees; but C.J. could not see these swatches of sky from where he sat) and there were the sounds of night creatures. And of a wind developing.

It was this—the wind—that made C.J. stiffen and become afraid. It was a cold wind, and he had to hug himself to stay warm, even inside his little leafy dome. The wind sent feelers through the leaves and made him cold.

The sound of the leaves turning over made him suddenly afraid, too. It was a sound that should have been comforting, but wasn't, a sound that should have soothed him, but instead made him cast about in the darkness for an unseen and anonymous enemy whose movements would be masked by the noises the wind made.

The doctor accepted the blanket from the orderly and noted in passing its musty odor.

Marie's eyes could make day out of the darkness, and could transform a landscape that was bathed in sunlight into a place of shadows.

She saw the light that wolves see, light no human has ever seen, because the universe was a place of light and darkness and shadows, and she was a creature of the universe, a creature prodded and pulled and thrown by the winds of creation. Winds that had blown for ten billion years.

Sometimes she was at the mercy of these winds.

Sometimes she rode them.

But she did not control them.

She walked in the forest where C.J. huddled in his leafy dome and she saw bright shafts of yellow light that were the spaces between trees, and columns of sullen darkness that were the trees themselves.

And above, through breaks in the canopy created by the trees, her eyes could have shown her, if she had looked, a white blanket of light, the stuff of the universe—stars and nebulae and galaxies overlapping one another a million times.

She walked as if she were human. It was her choice, to be as human as that—to walk in close approximation to the way humans walked, and to make love the way that humans made love. To conceive the way humans did. She was as human as she chose to be.

She walked with consummate grace. Naked arms and naked legs and naked torso moving in gentle rhythm.

She walked through the dark forest as if she were dancing.

And the violence within her was like heat.

C.J. did not hear her. She was close to him, and her footfalls on the soft forest floor were only as loud as a leaf turning over in the wind. He hugged himself for warmth inside his leafy dome, and he drew solace from the darkness, because he supposed that it hid him.

THIRTY-TWO

Six Years Earlier

Lisa Brown, Joanna's closest friend, says to Miles, "What you have here, Miles, in this house, is an angry, malevolent, and violent demon."

Miles gives her a condescending smile, but does not reply.

Lisa says, "I know you don't want to believe that, I know that the . . ." She pauses. ". . . academic mind wants everything quantified and qualified and pigeonholed, and some things really *can't* be, you understand."

"I understand that as much as anyone," Miles says.

"We both do," says Joanna.

"But," says Miles, "I'm afraid that we simply do not share your beliefs, Lisa."

C.J., who's standing nearby, thinks this is a very strange statement from his father. After all, his mom and dad had been talking a couple of days earlier about the strange hissing noises in the house, and they had said that these noises were "hard to account for," and that Lisa might be able to "throw light on the situation." But now C.J.'s dad is acting like Lisa is *loony,* not simply weird.

* * *

In the darkness inside his leafy dome, C.J. felt a wave of heat pass by and he strained to see through breaks in the leaves.

He saw Marie.

She was bending over, looking in at him.

Her face was inches away from his, her eyes were ablaze. She grinned a kind of mad, open-mouthed grin, and heat came from inside her, wafted into his little shelter, and took his breath away.

He screeched, threw himself backward, so his arms supported him from behind, and crabwalked backward, away from her.

He saw her too well in the darkness. She blazed.

He screeched again, and then broke through the other side of the dome, into the forest, and saw, through the leaves, into the shelter he had exited, that Marie was coming after him.

"Miles?" Lorraine said; she was sitting on her haunches in front of him in the walk-in closet. She reached out, touched him very lightly, shook her head, confused. "Miles," she said, "you're so cold." She paused. "Why are you so cold, Miles?"

He made no response. His out-of-focus gaze was on the area of her shoulder.

Lorraine reached for one of her winter coats, hanging nearby, so she could cover him and make him warm again.

THIRTY-THREE

WHAT HAPPENED THE DAY
AARON GOT LOST

The day that Dad brought Marie home for me to meet the first time it was warm and it was going to rain, I could hear the thunder, like buildings falling a long way away.

"He brought her home to meet me and she said, 'How are you, C.J.? What does that stand for?'

" 'Christopher Jonathan,' I said to her.

"And she said, 'It's a beautiful name. You should be called "Christopher," I think.'

"And my dad said, 'He prefers C.J.'

"She stayed overnight that night and I could hear her and my dad together in my dad and mom's bed, and it made me cry, and it made me scared, too.

"I woke up and heard the hissing noise that night, when Dad and Marie were quiet and it was late. I think that the hissing noise made me wake up. It was different than before. It was softer, like a whisper.

"Then it *was* a whisper, and it said, 'Christopher Jonathan, I am here!' and I looked and there was a long whitish

thing standing in the dark near my bed. It didn't look like
anything. It looked like water that has no place to go. Then
it got arms on it, then legs, and a head, and then a face. My
mother's face. Smiling. She said, 'Christopher Jonathan, I
am here!' And she reached out her arms to me in the dark.

"I was afraid. I didn't think it was my mom. I didn't
know. I *wanted* it to be my mom. I reached up to her, I
wanted her to hold me, and I said, 'Mom?'

"She leaned over and I reached farther for her. She got
me, and her hands went around my back. She pulled me off
the bed and hugged me. She was warm and smelled like my
mom. I liked it. I thought, *My mom is back!* I smiled into
her skin like I had a lot of times before.

"I stopped smiling because I couldn't breathe. She was
holding me close to her, the way she used to. She always
held me very close to her skin, like she was doing now. And
I could always breathe even with my face into her skin. But
now I had my face into her skin and I couldn't breathe, I
couldn't talk, either. She was so strong, she held me so tight,
and I got pictures in my mind of being all alone and not
breathing. No Dad or Mom. All alone, forever. No house
and no Matchbox cars and no breathing and no thoughts
or memories, like a thing that is buried in the earth, in the
dark, and the days pass and the trees change color and
winter comes and the snow falls and spring and summer
come, and there this thing in the earth is all the while, alone
and without memories or thoughts, but *knowing* that it is
alone and *knowing* that it has not always *been* alone. It
wants to cry it's so sad, but it can't cry. It has no eyes. It
used to have eyes but they're gone. And it has no mouth,
either. It is only a thing that fills up with sadness because it
knows about hands touching it, so it felt good, but it doesn't
remember them. And it knows about people around it, too,

and these people smiled and said nice things, but it does not *remember* them, either. And it knows about food in its mouth that tasted good and made hunger go away. It is always hungry now. It is always blind. It is always lonely. And it stays that way for all time, until the stars go out and never come back. Then it drifts about in the empty universe feeling hungry and sad and alone.

"Then I was back in the bed suddenly. My room had no hissing noise in it anymore. It was only dark.

"And there was a laugh coming at me from down the hall. It was Marie. She was laughing. She was doing it very quietly, so no one could hear.

"But *I* could hear her."

The first rays of morning sunlight cut through the trees and woke Miles. He raised his hand to shield his eyes and grunted his disenchantment.

He remembered the night, remembered the screeches—they had come from far away, he thought. An animal. Some bird that screeches. There were birds like that—birds that screeched. It had been some kind of . . . bird. Something with wings. Something that flew.

The night had been filled with creatures that flew. He had heard them, had felt them pass just above his head, had been stung by them—his body was alive with stings and bites, his bare chest and the area around his genitals especially, though he didn't know why this should be. He saw that his sweat was heaviest in these areas, but that fact meant nothing to him.

He stood, still shielding his eyes from the morning sunlight that cut through the trees. These words escaped him; "Mama, oh!" He heard the words, wondered about them, then they were gone forever.

He felt as if he were being emptied, as if he had been bloated, full, and now was not, now was emaciated, a thing nearly without substance, nearly a shadow.

He remembered that there had been a house. He could not remember what the house looked like, only that he had been inside it and that there had been other creatures inside it with him. And he remembered that there had been an apparition in the house with him, too.

And something else. Something more real. Something that spoke, or had tried to.

But now there was no house. There was only the forest, the morning sunlight, the cool air. There were little, irregularly shaped swatches of sky above, the smell of pine tar and damp earth, the soft touch of the forest floor against the soles of his feet.

"C.J.!" he yelled, but he had no idea what it meant or why he was yelling it.

He yelled it again. "C.J.!" And again. "C.J.!" And again. "C.J.! C.J.!"

He called "C.J.!" continuously for a long, long time. He didn't stop to listen for an answer each time he called it because he had no idea why he was calling it. It was as spontaneous as a sneeze.

He stopped calling the name suddenly and stayed quiet for a moment. Then he yelled, "Slow down or you'll hurt yourself." He yelled this for a very long time, too, until his throat hurt. He hardly stopped for a breath. Then he stopped yelling it and stayed quiet, while his brain spun with errant memories. Then he yelled, "Harvey died, he got run over!" There was a mental picture attendant to this; it was a picture of a large, reddish dog lying very still. Its tongue was hanging out, its eyes were half open, it had an awful bleeding wound in its side.

And when he was done yelling "Harvey died, he got run over!" he stayed quiet while his brain threw random bits of memory about, and he latched onto one—the way a drowning man latches onto a piece of driftwood—and he yelled, "Jo, do you want pancakes this morning?"

C.J. was miles away, but he heard his father. Sound traveled with wonderful ease through the thick, still atmosphere of the forest.

C.J. didn't hear individual words. He heard what sounded like the distant and noncontinuous humming of bees.

He listened closely.

He heard something achingly familiar in the sound he was hearing, in its pitch and urgency.

But he did not dare yell back for fear that the woman following might hear him. He had not seen her since dawn, a long time ago, and he hoped that he had outdistanced her. He'd always been a good runner, and he had never run so fast and so hard as he had run the previous night.

He was at the edge of a steep hill that was bare of trees, except at the bottom, almost a mile off, where there was a small stand of pines. The lake lay just beyond the pines.

Frontenac Island was much farther down the lake. It was visible only as a grayish-brown lump at this distance.

C.J. stared longingly at it.

He looked back, into the forest, fully expecting to see the woman with the wide grin and the blazing eyes there.

Marie!

Marie? he wondered.

Marie. The woman with the wide grin and the blazing eyes. The woman who had followed him through most of the night, keeping a good distance, but always visible, a point of hot light in the darkness.

"Marie," he whispered.

He remembered.

Of course.

He remembered *everything*.

He started down the steep slope toward the lake. The late morning sky was cloudless and dark blue, the sunlight on the hillside warm and reassuring.

When he was a hundred yards down the slope, he looked back, at the forest. A breeze stirred the pines.

He turned his head, looked at the lake, again. He saw movement far below, at the perimeter of the small stand of deciduous trees. He looked closely, saw nothing, stopped walking. The slope was precipitous here and he had to lean far back and support himself with his hands to keep from pitching forward or sliding down the slope on his rear end.

There was no vegetation other than saw grass between him and the stand of trees far below, and he thought that whoever was there could see him. He wanted suddenly to go back up the slope and into the forest. The slope was too open, he was too visible on it.

He began to cry. He fought the tears, but they came anyway.

"Dammit!" he whispered. How could he *see* anything if he was crying?

"There," Lorraine soothed as she put her winter coat over Miles's bare shoulders. "You'll be warmer, now. You'll be all right." She looked silently at him for a long while. He was very ill, that was clear. She needed to go and call someone immediately.

But she thought that if she did that, he wouldn't be here when she got back.

She thought that he was . . . fading even as she watched. As if what she was looking at was not *him* but only her very clear and nightmarishly transient *memory* of him.

So she was afraid to leave him, even for a moment, though she knew that it was necessary.

She reached, touched his cheek. So cold. So . . . transparent. There was the skull beneath the skin. The eye sockets. The rictus grin.

"Oh, Miles," she whimpered, "don't leave us. Please, please don't leave us."

Miles did not reply.

THIRTY-FOUR

C. J. hadn't eaten in over a day. It surprised him. It was a surprise to feel hunger pangs. It was a surprise, too, when he realized that he had to pee.

Through the day, he had made his way slowly, and with great caution, across the tree line at the top of the slope that paralleled the lake, to an area not far above Frontenac Island. The island drew him because it was so familiar—it was the *only* thing familiar in this place.

He relieved himself against the trunk of a sumac and noted his reddish, elongated shadow as he peed. He was at the center of a small and sparse grove of deciduous trees, and the sun setting through wispy high cirrus clouds turned shadows a rich rust-red.

He repositioned himself so he would not see the shadow of his urine stream.

He thought about his hunger when he was done peeing. He knew that there were edible flowers about, and berries of various kinds—raspberries, elderberries, blueberries. He had seen them on his way here. And he thought, too, that he could try to fish, but quickly realized that that would mean fashioning a hook, somehow, and then, if he caught something, building a fire. He had no idea how to fashion a hook, no idea what he would use for fishing line, and no idea how he would build a fire without matches.

Fishing was out.

The rust-red shadows of the trees turned darker suddenly, and then were gone as the sun sank behind the far hills. C.J. realized that he would have to wait until morning to concentrate on satisfying his hunger.

Refuse middens, he thought. His brow furrowed. What were refuse middens? They sounded like something you put on your hands to take out the garbage.

The night was going to be a cold. Already, the still air was cool enough to raise goose bumps on his exposed arms. He would have to find some sort of shelter here, in this little stand of trees. Perhaps he could find something similar to the leafy dome he had used the previous evening. But when he thought about it, it didn't seem likely that he'd find anything like that here—this stand of trees seemed too young and strong.

Perhaps he could fashion a lean-to, somehow. Break off thin branches and pile them up against the trunk of a tree. He'd seen it done.

When had he seen it done? he wondered.

He thought about it for a long time, and, at last, he remembered. He had seen it done a year and a half ago when he and his father and Aaron had walked the Cayuga Nature Trail after some Boy Scouts or Girl Scouts or Camp Fire kids had been through a day earlier. They—the Boy Scouts—had done that, they'd built lean-tos out of fallen tree branches.

Aaron? he wondered.

"My brother," he whispered.

He heard movement in the underbrush nearby. He started, looked, saw nothing because of the darkness.

Marie! he thought. He saw her in his memory. She was a
mist, a thing with his mother's face, a thing that suffocated,
a moving point of light in the darkness. She was breasts and
nakedness.

He smelled her.

He had always enjoyed her smell, and then, because he
hated her, had hated it. He was aware of her smell, now. He
wasn't sure if it was a real smell, or only his memory of it.

He could not see her face in his memory. He saw his
mother's face. He saw her leaning over his bed. Saw her
reaching for him. Heard her crooning to him, "Christopher
Jonathan, I am here."

But his mother had always called him C.J.

It was Marie who had called him Christopher Jonathan.

Aaron? he wondered. *Who is Aaron?* He thought about
for it a moment and whispered, "He's is my half brother."
How could he have forgotten that? If only for a minute.

He remembered *everything*.

He knew all at once that he was afraid. Afraid because he
was beginning to forget, and he had forgotten nothing his
entire life.

"Christopher Jonathan," he heard, and he wheeled about
to face the person speaking to him. "Christopher Jonathan.
I am here."

"Who is it?" he shouted.

But the darkness showed him nothing.

Miles had begun to whisper, because his voice was nearly
gone. "I've seen things you people wouldn't believe," he
whispered. "Attack ships on fire off the shoulder of Orion."
They were lines from a movie he had watched more times
than he could remember, when he was remembering anything.

Blackflies had settled on him. He was sitting up against the trunk of a tree, and his arms were at his sides, palms up, his chin at the top of his chest, eyes half open. The flies were concentrating on his moist areas. He saw the flies and noted them, but only in the way that a camera would, without comprehension, or passion. The flies bit him and enjoyed themselves; he felt a momentary pain, forgot it, then there was pain again.

The images that attended the lines he whispered—images from the movie he had seen more times than he could remember—were of a tall blond android who was hunched over at the top of a rundown building in a dark, polluted, and rainy San Francisco of the not-too-distant future. In every sense that mattered, the android was human. But it had been programmed to come to the end of its existence at a given moment. This was that moment—its time to die.

"Time to die," Miles whispered, again and again, barely pausing for breath; it was a line from the same movie. He whispered the words but did not recognize them or realize that he was whispering them.

The blackflies gorged themselves as he spoke.

Dusk came. All around him, the trees merged into the gray twilight. The blackflies flew away.

Miles whispered now, " 'Officious little prick.' " He whispered the words again and again. They were part of the first line of one of his favorite novels. " 'Officious little prick,' he whispered in a monotone. " 'Officious little prick.' "

The orderly said, "The heat's been fixed, Doc."

The doctor glanced over at him. "Maintain it at its present level. We've got to keep this child warm."

The other doctor, standing nearby, grinned in confusion, and said, "He's . . . like an apparition. What's happening to him, for Christ's sake? What's *happening* to him?"

The first doctor shook his head. "I don't know."

<u>THIRTY-FIVE</u>

L orraine asked herself how long it would take her, after
all, to go into the bedroom, call 911, and tell them to
send an ambulance? Twenty seconds?

But she did not move from Miles's side. She couldn't. She
thought that if she left him, for however brief a time, that
he would be gone when she returned and that no matter
how long she looked, she would not find him again.

Aaron Gale loved his mother very much. He loved the
feel of her, the smell of her, the look of her. He longed for
her when she wasn't around. He thought about her and
needed her more than he needed anything else.

It was a longing that she had cultivated, because she
needed him, too.

She was alone without him.

He was her creation. Just as *she* had been a creation of the
universe, he was *her* creation, and she was very possessive
of him, and he of her.

So when she had disappeared, he had fallen into a depression so deep that it had nearly killed him.

After her disappearance, he slept for days, and could not
be awakened. Miles had taken him, asleep, to his pediatrician, who had declared that the problem was very likely

neurological, and that Aaron should be admitted to the hospital—where the pediatrician kept his office—at once for tests.

But Aaron awoke, and because he appeared to be physically well, his admission to the hospital was postponed.

Miles tried to talk with his son, tried to coax him back to what he—Miles—saw as the real world. But Aaron remained sullen and uncommunicative for months.

And he continued to sleep most of the day and night.

Miles watched him as he slept, and guessed—from Aaron's whispering, cooing, smiles, frowns, and occasional weeping—that the boy had developed a comforting and reassuring dreamworld to inhabit. A dreamworld also inhabited by his mother, Marie.

Miles was right about this. Aaron *did* have a dreamworld to inhabit. But it was unlike any dreamworld that any other child had ever inhabited.

It was real.

It had been real.

It would be real.

It was a place of birth, and death, and rebirth. A place of light, and darkness, of stasis, and of anarchy. A place of awesome silence, of screeching, and laughter, and orgasmic whispers. A place that was *all* times and *all* places, *all* creation, and all dissolution. A place that was immense and tiny and nondimensional, a place that smelled of earth and water, a place that carried whole planets in pants pockets, a place where the groaning dead played children's games, and grew, and grew, and learned to speak in several languages, and loved, and had babies, and learned to run. A place of atmospheres and magma and hydrogen atoms, a place where bony fingers flexed and moving water made

canyons out of rock, and clocks ticked, and the elderly
wailed like infants, and grain held within it the stuff of
galaxies.

A place that was the first moment of time that was all of
time.

The place that had built his mother up and thrown her
into itself, into history.

The place that Aaron dreamed of in those days after the
winds took his mother from him.

The place she had shown him.

The place of her birth.

Miles was silent, finished with the phrase that had occupied him now for so long—"Officious little prick." His
brain had used it up, and so, in this place and time, the
phrase was gone forever.

His brain churned up another phrase, from a book that
he had read more times than he could remember. That
phrase was, "Cold fell over the Inn like the news of a
death." Miles whispered this phrase again and again.

And around him, in the cool darkness, the people gath-
ered cautiously. Although their eyes showed them little
more than shadows, they watched him, and they listened to
him in awe. And slowly, they drew closer to him.

Aaron was naked and cold.

His mother kept him naked because she stayed naked.
Temperature had no effect on her and she assumed it had
no effect on her son. She assumed that her son was precisely
what she was. But temperature did affect him, because he
was *not* precisely what she was. He was human, because his
father had been human, and because his mother—Marie—
had *become* human to give him birth.

This was a fact that she had overlooked.

She overlooked much.

She had hidden him in a clearing, under the towering, broad crown of a live oak tree that the Laurentian people shunned because it was a place that she inhabited.

She was now, for them, a creature to be avoided more than the icy cold, or the black, swirling summer storms, or the sudden rains that made small streams into killing floods.

She had arrived on the winds that blew in six directions at the same time. The winds that could make a man become his insides. The winds that blew all at once, without warning, and took members of the tribe away forever.

She had arrived on these winds, and had looked to be one of the tribe—short, stocky, muscular, dark-skinned, broad-nosed, high cheekboned. But she also appeared to be a *rider* of the winds, and so she was clearly one with the Great Spirit. Someone to be revered.

And then, on a midsummer's day, under a broiling sun, she had left them, carried away by the same awful winds.

And had returned almost at once, changed, unrecognizable, and heavy with child.

She had given birth to the child, then had left them again.

And now, in the eyes of the Laurentian people, she was as evil a creature as had ever existed. More evil, even, than the winds themselves because she could *direct* her hatred.

She caused the screaming death with only a glance. The people were sure of it. (How many had died since she had returned? As many as could be counted on the fingers of both hands? More? No one knew precisely. Some to whom the screaming death came went off by themselves to die.)

And so, they did not even dare look at her.

And now her son from another place hunched up cold

and confused and very human beneath the live oak where she had put him, in the clearing where the Laurentian people would not go.

Marie was laughing. It sounded like a screech.

C.J. had never before heard such laughter from her. She had not laughed that way when she'd lived in the same house with him. She had laughed the way he had often heard adults laugh, with control; but the laughter he had heard from her had sometimes been a strange kind of hiccoughing laughter, as if she were unaccustomed to it, as if it were something foreign to her.

This screeching laughter—like an animal in a frenzy of pain or pleasure—seemed truer and more natural. It made him cringe and it made him very afraid.

He could see her. She was a column of diffuse light. She was naked, yellow. Her face looked oversized, too big for her body. Distorted. And, as she laughed, her mouth twisted into huge, irregular ovals and her eyes shut so tightly they were nearly invisible.

He could see only her. She commanded all of his attention. She was his universe, his time. She was his past, his future, his present.

He could smell her—the odor of earth and water, the smell he loved and despised at the same time because it was *her* smell. And he could feel her, could feel her heat, and it was so overwhelming it made him perspire.

"I am *everything!*" she screeched at him through her laughter.

And he knew that, for him, here, it was true.

He ran from her, into the darkness.

He hit a tree almost at once and the collision knocked

him down, onto his back. He closed his eyes in sudden pain and shock. "Shit!" he screamed.

He felt her heat. He smelled her—the odor of earth and water.

He opened his eyes. She was above him, within arm's reach—her huge face and distorted mouth and eyes so tightly shut he could hardly see them.

He lashed out at her. His fist connected with her cheek. She straightened suddenly, as if in surprise.

He scrambled to his feet and continued running. He was beyond the stand of trees now. There was a slope above and it led to the forest. Below, it led to the lake, and Frontenac Island.

He looked back, toward the stand of trees he had just come out of. He was breathless, dizzy, on the verge of tears because of his fear.

He saw her. She was standing quietly, yellow eyes intent on him, just at the edge of the stand of trees.

THIRTY-SIX

Aaron Gale cried out, "Mama, Mama!" because the darkness confused him and terrified him; there were strange shapes and smells and sounds in it.

"Mama!" he cried.

This wasn't his home. His home was with C.J., and with his father. And his mother. But even she—whom he loved more than anything, and who had brought him here—had abandoned him.

(He remembered the car door opening, remembered dropping his *Masters of the Universe* comic book, remembered reaching for it, clutching it, feeling a strong hand on his arm, looking, seeing his mother's face, seeing trees beyond her.)

"Mama!" he cried, but his voice was lost in the dark, in the trees, was covered by the sounds of the creatures moving around him.

There were people nearby. He could see them—they were squat, silent shadows, and they moved with an odd kind of grace on short, thick legs.

They moved slowly, but unhaltingly.

And Aaron wanted to see their eyes. He could see only their squat, dark shapes, not their faces, not their eyes. Faces were everything. Faces showed love, anger, intention.

He drew his knowledge of the world and of his place in it from faces. The face of his mother, his father, his brother, strangers.

But these creatures had no faces in the dark. They were little more than the dark. They were the dark moving.

"Mama!" he cried.

"Ma . . mah!" came the reply.

C.J. made it up the slope to the forest before looking back. He didn't stop running. He craned his head around for an instant and looked down the slope to where he had been. He saw Marie, halfway up the slope. She was only a yellowish, elongated glow in the darkness and he merely glanced at her, not long enough to see how fast she was moving, or, indeed, if she was still moving at all. He remembered hitting the tree—his forehead was a knot of pain—so he looked back at the forest almost at once to avoid hitting another.

He ran for half a minute; his eyes were accustomed to the darkness and he avoided the trees easily.

He saw a white light far ahead. He slowed. As he watched, the light grew rapidly larger.

He stopped running.

The single light became two lights. He stared at them, fascinated. He knew such lights as these. He'd seen them before, many times.

When? he wondered. But he couldn't remember.

He heard a distant low humming noise that came from the direction of the two lights.

The humming noise became a low growl and the lights stabbed at him so he had to look away.

The low growl grew louder, and, at last, he realized what the lights were and what the growling noise was.

This was a *car* approaching, an *automobile (brand-new Celebrity Eurosport, front wheel drive, crushed velvet seats, '57 Chevy Impala, straight eight overdrive).*

And the car approaching was almost upon him.

Twin halogens, split grill—

He leaped to his right seconds before the car shot past, horn blaring.

And he landed on his stomach in a shallow ditch that was heavy with tall weeds and stinging nettle. The nettle had brushed his face, neck and hands, and he howled now from the searing pain.

After a few moments he stopped howling and merely whimpered. He brushed his fingers against his cheek and neck; welts had risen. He touched them lightly, in his mind's eye could see the welts—irregularly shaped white splotches surrounded by red. This was not his first encounter with stinging nettle (*"Urtica dioisa,* member of the *Urticaceae* family, found in most parts of the continental United States, contains formic acid) . . .

Not far off, a dog began to bark. Carefully, so as not to touch the stinging nettle again, C.J. pushed himself to his feet. He saw no trees. There was a hillside in front of him, but it was bare, apparently—he couldn't be certain in the moonlit dark.

He looked up, surprised to see a cloudless sky and a half moon (diameter 2,126 miles, first explored, in a very limited way, July 20, 1969 by astronauts Neil Armstrong, and Michael Collins—).

"Shit!" he breathed. Why couldn't he keep these errant facts from bubbling over?

He turned around. The creamy moonlight reflected from the asphalt surface of a road just in front of him. At the opposite shoulder of the road, a barking dog stood motionless. It was a large dog; it had a black body and a white snout—that much was visible in the dim moonlight—and its bark was quick, a warning; *Stay away from my side of the road!* it said ("Wolves have a complex series of gestures to indicate dominance, submission, fear, anger. Dogs, being closely related to wolves—").

C.J. heard another car approaching far to his right. He looked. The car's headlights bathed an area a quarter-mile off in a hazy light. *Ground fog,* he realized.

The dog's barking quickened and became higher in pitch.

"Why am I here?" C.J. whispered.

He felt pressure on his shoulder, as if a hand had been laid there.

The dog's barking grew frantic.

C.J. whirled around.

He saw a soft spray of moonlight on the weeds and stinging nettle around him; he saw the dark gray bulk of the bare hillside beyond, the Big Dipper above.

The air was cold, damp. He shivered. "Dammit!" he muttered, and hugged himself.

He felt fingers touch him at the top of his spine. He stiffened. The fingers worked their way down to his lower back, then started up his spine again.

He heard a chuckle, quick and strangely distant.

Behind him, the dog's frantic barking became a low growl, threatening and insistent.

C.J. shivered again. He heard the dog lunge forward, its claws scrabbling on the asphalt.

He turned quickly, looked. The dog stepped back and lowered its head. Its eyes gleamed dully with moonlight.

"Marie," C.J. whispered. He did not see her. He saw only the dog, the moonlight, the asphalt.

"Weak child," Marie whispered. "Do you like the wind?"

He felt a hand on his back. It pushed him forward, onto the road.

The dog lunged again. It stopped almost at once, only a foot away, and lowered its head menacingly.

"Do you *like* the *wind!*" Marie screeched. He felt her hand on his back again. He tensed. She pushed. She was far too strong. He could not resist. He went forward. The dog lunged.

"Bullshit!" Marie screeched, and C.J. felt the dog's teeth sink into his skin.

The doctor said, "That's very fanciful. But I'm afraid you're wrong, Doctor. This child is not 'like an apparition.' He's real, he's in trouble, and we're here to help him. If you insist on making fanciful, unprofessional comments, I must ask you to leave."

Miles saw two horizontal lines coming together in darkness. There was nothing above the lines or below them, beyond them, or in front of them. The lines were all that his existence was made of, and they were slowly closing, slowly coming together. An arm's width of darkness separated them now.

He could not feel the fingers that prodded him, caressed him, pinched him, stroked him. And he could not hear the guttural voices that made unintelligible expressions of awe and wonderment and confusion. He could not see the broad, flat faces, and the small, wide-set dark eyes that peered at him. And he could not see the sun—rust-red through low, wispy clouds—as it rose through the trees.

He was beyond all that.

The horizontal lines converged in the darkness. They bulged where they joined and a light formed there.

Soon, the horizontal lines were gone and only a pinpoint of dull light remained.

THIRTY-SEVEN

Lorraine thought, *He's vanishing. Everything he is is going away.* His ideas, his needs, his desires, his hungers; everything that made him Miles Gale was slipping into nothingness. It was the awful fact of *him* that made her think this way—the cold skin, the skull and eye sockets and rictus grin so horribly visible beneath.

"Don't leave us, Miles," she whimpered, and touched his cheek lingeringly with her fingertips.

C.J.'s forearm bore two pairs of bright red marks—one above, one below—where the dog had gotten hold of him. C.J. touched the marks on the upper side of his forearm. "Huh?" he said. He did not remember the encounter with the dog. He remembered the scrabbling noise that the dog's feet had made on the asphalt, the ground fog lit by a distant car's headlights, the dark, bare hillside. But these were disconnected memories, as if recalled from other, distant times in his life.

As he watched, the bright red marks on his forearm became bright pink, then only slightly pinker than his skin. Soon, they were gone, and he forgot them.

He looked about. The forest was hazy with morning

light. The air was warm, the ground still cool from the cold evening; here and there, tendrils of mist rose.

Above, through a break in the pines, a large, silent, broad-beaked bird caught his eye. The bird's wide, dark wings beat slowly—the effort hardly seemed enough to keep it aloft—as the bird passed to the west and was soon obscured by trees.

Great blue heron, C.J. thought. He remembered what herons were. He'd seen them many times. He was happy for the memory.

When? he wondered. When had he seen herons?

He tried to remember. "With my father," he whispered at last. "At the lake with my father."

This pleased him, too. He smiled. He stopped smiling.

At the lake with my father wasn't enough. What lake? What damned lake? He didn't know. His memory showed him a lake—long, and narrow, and very blue. It was known for its "fathomless depths." And, like all lakes, it had a name. But he couldn't remember it. He remembered other names. "Marie," "Aaron," "Celebrity," "Triphammer." But he thought that these names had nothing to do with lakes. Or did they? He wasn't sure.

He couldn't *remember!*

He began to weep because his incredible memory was beginning to fail him.

Nearby, a squirrel on the lowest branch of a red pine scolded him for breaking the morning's lazy silence.

The doctor standing near the bed in the warm room said, "I'm sorry. It's just very . . . astonishing, it's very bizarre—" She paused meaningfully. "Yes, you're right. I will attempt to behave more professionally."

* * *

Aaron Gale peered intently into his mother's face as she scooped him up and held him close. He got a momentary look at her before his own face was above her shoulder and he was looking behind her, seeing, to his left, at the periphery of his vision, her dark hair; below, her smooth dark back and buttocks; to his right, a ragged line of young pines; and ahead, the clearing.

Marie cooed to him as she held him, "My boy, my son, my little one."

He paid no attention to her words. He paid no attention to the pines. He remembered looking into her eyes as she had scooped him up. Throughout the cold night without her, he had needed her, had needed her face, her eyes, her comfort.

But there had been nothing in her eyes in the moment just passed to give him comfort. Only darkness.

He pushed himself away from her suddenly, so she was holding him by his legs, and his hands were flat against the top of her bare chest and his arms were straight. He peered hard into her eyes. She peered back, yellow eyes unblinking, pupils contracted to black dots.

He saw nothing. Her eyes were blank. There was no comfort in them. There was no comfort in her face.

He didn't think about any of this. Her face and eyes had given him comfort all his life. But they gave him nothing, now. He did not note the difference, did not think about it. He only stared at her and felt very empty, and very alone.

"My son, my little one," Marie cooed, and her voice was full of the same kind of love and comfort for him that it had always been.

But her face was blank and her eyes were empty, passionless.

He continued staring at her.

She stared back.

She saw a thousand of him. One.

"My precious boy," she cooed.

He hit her on the shoulder with his fist. He had decided all at once that this was not his mother. This was somebody who *acted* like his mother, but was someone else.

She did not feel the blow.

"My boy, my son, my little one," she cooed.

He hit her again, and again, and again. He rained blows on her with his small fists. But she did not notice. She saw a thousand of him, one. She broke the movements of his fists up into bits of noncontinuous reality. She put the movement together, made it into *time,* made it into *substance,* disregarded it.

"My precious boy," she cooed.

Tendrils of mist rose around them from the cool green earth into the warm morning air.

She pulled him close and held him very tightly. She was incredibly strong. "My boy, my son, my little one," she cooed.

He smelled her, the familiar earthy smell that pleased him so much.

Then he did not smell her because he couldn't breathe. She was holding him too tightly.

He hit her on the cheek with his fist. "No, Mommy, no!" he pleaded; suddenly, she was indeed his mother again, she *had* to be his mother; he could only plead successfully with his mother, who, beneath this stiff mask of passionless power, still loved him. He could not plead with an imposter.

"No!" he wheezed, and hit her again.

"My son," she cooed, "my little one." And held him tighter.

"No!" he whispered.

She let go of him.

He dropped.

He hit the soft earth with a dull thud; his rear end hit first, then his back, his arms, his head.

He stared up at her, tried hard to catch his breath.

She looked back at him, her eyes expressionless, as if she were looking at a leaf that had fallen.

"Mommy?" Aaron whispered.

Her mouth fell open a little, as if the muscles there had suddenly become detached from her jaw. Her unfocused gaze shifted so she was looking slightly above his eyes, now, so she was looking somewhere in the vicinity of his forehead.

Aaron looked confusedly at her. Suddenly, this woman was again someone he didn't know, the approximation of his mother, a thing made of clay.

Her gaze shifted again; it was a slow, lazy movement, as if her eye muscles had become detached.

He heard a wind start. It signaled itself in the trees, began as a low rushing sound which grew rapidly louder; the tall grasses around him bent over and his long hair blew across his face so he could not see.

The wind was as cold as deep winter, and Aaron drew himself up into the fetal position to protect himself from it.

Above him, Marie cooed, "My boy, my son, my little one." He heard her as if she were speaking from a great distance.

He looked at her.

Her gaze was on him again.

And her eyes were the eyes he remembered—full of love and comfort and caring.

"Mommy!" he screamed, against the cold, against the

wind, so she would hear him and sweep him into her arms
again, and hold him, protect him.

Her gaze shifted once more.

Her jaw fell open.

"Mommy!" he screamed, wanting her to come back to
him, wanting this stranger, this *thing* to go away.

"My boy, my son," she cooed. "My little one."

He covered his eyes, drew himself into a ball, instinctively
protected his insides from the cold wind.

The wind stopped after a long while.

He looked.

His mother was gone.

Miles's world was made of light. There were no shadows
in it, no textures, no gradations. Only light.

The people touching him, prodding him, pinching him
were losing interest and were slowly drifting off.

A few remained. A man who was taller and leaner than
the others. A woman who was the man's mate and who
found Miles's body endlessly fascinating. It was so white, so
hairless, so thin and weak-looking.

She touched her mate to get his attention, nodded at
Miles's thigh, then grabbed it; her large dark hand nearly
half-encircled it.

She smiled at her mate.

He chuckled. The sound was low and harsh but oddly
musical, as if he chuckled quite a lot.

Miles's world was made of light.

He knew nothing of these people and their amusement in
him.

He knew only the light.

No memories whispered at him, prodded him, piqued his
emotions. The light was forever.

He *was* the light.

The attention of the man and woman looking at him was diverted by the screams of one of the other men, who had wandered off with the others. The scream was an extended scream of pain and confusion, just the kind of scream that the man and woman had heard again and again in the past month.

THIRTY-EIGHT

C. J. heard the man scream, although the distance was considerable, and his first impulse was to run toward it. But he thought better of this after a few paces. He stopped running.

He listened.

The scream continued, unbroken.

After a long while, it ended abruptly.

C.J. stood very still and waited for the scream to continue. He heard nothing.

He began to sweat and grow fearful because there had been something very disturbing about the scream. Screams could not possibly go on for whole minutes at a time, as this one had. The man must have been in awful pain, and the pain must have been caused by something more than just a broken arm, a knife wound, a toothache. The pain the man felt must have been caused by something that made all his nerves fire at once and overpower even his need to breathe.

What could possibly cause pain like that?

C.J. ran. Away from the direction of the scream. He didn't know what he was running toward. The interior of the forest. The lake. The Laurentian people.

And he didn't care.

* * *

A jumping spider hopped onto Aaron Gale's foot. He felt it, looked at it, wondered about it a moment. It was small and black and had a red mark on its back; its head moved left and right in a strange, mechanical way. Aaron kicked, and the spider was gone.

Aaron called for his mother.

He heard distant thunder in reply.

He called again.

He heard thunder again, closer, louder. The sky was clear, and the air was still and warm. This seemed to Aaron to be a strange atmosphere for a storm.

He called for his mother again—"Mama!"—and saw movement at the perimeter of the forest, near the edge of the clearing. But it was short-lived and Aaron thought it was probably just a bird hopping from one branch to another, as he had so often seen birds do on the big tree outside his window at home. He was right about this. What he had seen now was only a young bluejay hopping about, happy for the warmth after a cold night, and a little agitated and restless, too, because of the coming storm.

Aaron's mother was nowhere in sight and this was not a situation that he dealt with well. For most of his six years, his mother had been nearby, almost always within view, when he needed her. She had become, in this way, a part of him, and a part of his strength in dealing with an uncertain world—for six years, the uncertain world of growing fitfully into his twos and threes and fours, the uncertain and unpredictable world of nursery school (which, complaining about the "adulterous influence of normal children," she had taken him out of after only two weeks), the uncertain world of the night and of going off to sleep. Then she had disappeared, and his strength had vanished. To his young eyes, the world that his brother and his father inhabited was wild and uncontrollable and malevolent. So he retreated from it.

Very slowly, he came back, although with an always-watchful and cautious eye. Then she had returned, had brought him here, had stayed with him. And now was gone again. And *this* world—even when she had been beside him—was indeed wild and unpredictable. Its people were people he did not recognize. His *mother* was someone he did not always recognize.

"Mama!" he screamed. But he was certain now that he was alone.

Miles existed in a world of light. His naked body lay on the forest floor; he was covered with goose bumps, though the air had become warm. And he existed in a world without color or gradations or textures, a world without movement or sound or memory. Only light. This was the beginning. Not the darkness, which always followed the light.

The others who had been prodding and pinching and poking and stroking him had gone off to watch in horror and helplessness the awful death of their neighbor, just as they had watched the deaths of so many in the past month.

The death had happened and the people were carrying the body to Frontenac Island for burial. They did not call it Frontenac Island. They called it, in their own tongue, *The place for the dead*.

It was a long way to the island, and much of the journey was accomplished in an eerie and fearful silence, although occasionally one of the people carrying the body shouted a word or a phrase that was common to the dead man, thus allowing the dead man to speak to his neighbors for the last time. He spoke, in this way, of the things which were important to him—of his mate, who followed at a good distance, as was the custom, of his child, a boy of five who waited at the village and knew nothing of the death of his father, of food he particularly enjoyed—venison and wild berries were his favorite—and, because the man had been one who laughed quite a lot and told funny stories, there were even a few of these.

Within two hours, while the sun was still far from setting, and the afternoon had become sticky and warm, the journey to the island—*The place for the dead*—was done, the body carried, held high aloft, through the shallow water, then dumped unceremoniously into a shallow grave; it shared space with dozens of other bodies recently buried there.

The man's soul had left him during the journey. What remained, his grotesquely pliant body, was, in effect, only so much garbage.

C.J.'s eyes filled with wonder as he looked at the high waterfalls above him.

The falls had literally taken him by surprise.

He had been following an idly moving stream—weary from his running, he had been wandering along the shore, against the stream's north-south current—and had been intent on watching the stream widen and become ever more furious and swift-moving. He hadn't noticed the freight train roar of the falls until he had rounded a rocky bend.

And there it was—one hundred feet of frothy water churning down at him and billowing into clouds of white spray within a dozen yards of where he stood. The wind that the falls created rippled his hair. He squinted against the spray as it soaked him to the skin.

"Ohhhh!" he shouted, straining his vocal cords with the

effort, trying to hear himself above the noise of the water. But he heard only the water.

He did not hear himself.

He thought that he should recognize these falls, as magnificent as they were. He thought he should know what name to call them. Some names flitted about in his memory. Niagara, Victoria, Taughanook. He wondered if these were the names of waterfalls, if these waterfalls were called Niagara, or Victoria, or Taughanook.

He couldn't remember.

He remembered *Celebrity, Impala, Aaron.* And he wondered if these, too, were the names of waterfalls.

He couldn't remember.

"Noooooo!" he shouted, and could not hear himself above the water and the wind.

THIRTY-NINE

Six Years Earlier

Lisa says, "Yes, a rather minor, ineffectual demon." She grins nervously, then continues, "And I don't know how to say this . . . hell, I don't even know where it comes from. But she—I keep saying 'she,' don't I?—isn't very . . . aware. Maybe that's not the right word. I think she's aware, as aware as she can be . . . I don't know. She's simply not very smart."

"Christ!" Miles mumbles.

"And I think," Lisa finishes, "that that could make her very, very dangerous."

The frothing white water filled C.J.'s vision and made him dizzy, afraid, desperate. He turned away from the waterfall and started back down the wide stream he had followed here.

Marie stood in his way. She was naked and smiling. Her smooth skin glistened from the spray of the waterfall.

C.J. stopped short. A small "Ah!" of surprise escaped him. Who was this woman? What did she want from him?

Marie said, "You look confused, weak child. You look

out of your depth." Her smile broadened. Her yellow eyes widened. She held her arms out to him. "Let me hold you and comfort you," she invited.

He stumbled backwards, away from her, toward the powerful, frothing water.

She advanced on him, arms extended, long black hair slick from the water, her smooth dark skin glistening.

C.J. shouted at her, "Don't touch me!"

"But I must," she told him.

He backed away more quickly, glanced behind him at the towering waterfall, closed his eyes against the fierce spray.

He turned his head back toward Marie, opened his eyes.

She was nearly upon him.

"Don't touch me!" he screamed.

"Let me embrace you, weak child!" she mouthed at him, her voice inaudible beneath the incredible rushing noise of the water.

He continued backing away from her, fearful of her embrace; he did not consciously remember the awful, deadening embrace of the creature who, so long ago, had pretended to be his mother.

This creature.

This demon.

He did not dare glance behind to see how close he had come to the waterfall; Marie was nearly touching him now; she was moving with exquisite and chilling grace through the white swirling mist—arms outstretched, yellow eyes wide with pleasure, mouth half-open in a grotesque half smile.

C.J. could barely stand. The winds here, near the base of the waterfall, were hurricane strength.

"Let me embrace you, weak child!" she mouthed.

"Don't—" C.J. started.

Her smile vanished.

She stopped moving forward.

Her stomach deflated suddenly, became concave, so the sharp outline of her ribs showed.

Her breasts flattened, her cheeks became hollow, her black hair, stringy from the water, swept back, her yellow eyes narrowed to slits.

She screamed.

C.J. heard the scream, despite the wind and water.

She screamed again. It was shrill, ragged, confused—the scream of an animal.

Then she spiraled off into the swirling mist like a mayfly in a windstorm.

Aaron's *Masters of the Universe* comic book had lain exposed to the weather for a couple of weeks, so its words and images were barely recognizable. But Aaron had memorized the entire comic book and while he held it gingerly in his hands, now—it threatened to crumble into nothingness if he held it too roughly—he saw the faded artwork in his memory, and heard the words in his head.

This was good. This was part of what was. And of what should be. A part of what he had been. A part of the time that his mother had pulled him from.

He hated her for that.

Hated her for putting him here, among people who did not speak to him, who only gawked from a safe distance. Hated her for making him afraid, and cold, and then making him warm, and secure. And then taking it all away.

Hated her for being a creature he did not recognize.

Hated her for being his mother.

For giving him birth.

FORTY

WHAT HAPPENED THE DAY
AARON GOT LOST

I was seven and Aaron was three and he was trying to tell me about a dream he had. I thought it was a dream. I didn't know, it *sounded* like a dream, but he couldn't talk well and so I couldn't figure out what he was saying, not all of it, anyway.

"He said that he was inside his mother in the dream. And that he was just about to be born. He said that she was not in the house, then, but that there were fields all around her, and woods around the fields, and a blue sky above. 'Boo sky,' he said.

"I said to him, 'But you were born in this house, Aaron. You were born in the closet.'

"He shook his head hard, like he meant it, and he said to me, 'No. No. I wasn't. I was borned out there.'

"I asked of him, 'Out where?'

"He waved his arms around and he said again, 'Out there! With those funny people around.' "

* * *

The storm had arrived unheralded by a squall line or by sudden, gusty winds. It happened as suddenly as a knock at the door, and it had the anger of devils in it.

Aaron ran from it, out of the clearing where his mother had put him so long ago, and into the surrounding and sheltering forest.

The storm followed, its fury muted only a little by the forest.

Around Aaron, the trees bent over like grass. The air became alive with branches and leaves and pine needles flung by the awful winds.

Aaron fell. Scrambled to his feet. Ran. Fell again.

The storm pursued him relentlessly through the forest.

He screamed.

The forest grew dark with the storm. He saw the trees as if they were ghosts and heard the wind bellowing its anger.

And he felt it wrap itself around him as if it were trying to suffocate him.

He closed his eyes, felt the debris of the wind-driven forest stinging him everywhere.

He screamed. He closed his eyes against the detritus of the storm.

And the wind felt like a pair of human hands on him. It lifted him by the shoulders and off the ground. It held him close to its foul-smelling breast; it grunted at him words he did not understand.

It soothed him.

He looked it in the face.

He gasped.

It chuckled quickly.

And carried him off.

* * *

Touching Miles's skin now was like touching thin paper. It was frightening to touch him. But Lorraine touched him, anyway. She let her fingers caress him very lightly; she was afraid he might crumble, might tear, might fall to pieces.

And yet he still breathed. She could see his lungs working. They were oblong shadows beneath the thin paper of his chest.

And his heart was a lump of moving darkness between his lungs.

She did not know what was happening to him.

She thought that the universe had turned upside down and inside out.

C.J. asked himself, "Where am I supposed to be?"

If not in this place, then where?

He didn't know.

He thought it was possible that he had always been here, in this forest, on these hills. Possible that he'd been born here, raised here, by people whose faces he couldn't remember, and whose voices he could not hear in his memory.

He didn't know.

Marie! he thought. He saw her in his mind's eye—she was a mist, a moving point of light in the darkness, she was breasts and nakedness.

He smelled her.

Who was she?

He didn't know.

Her smell was earthy, real, natural. He loved it. He despised it. It made him afraid.

He didn't know why.

What *did* he know? he wondered. Words and images flitted about in his head but he could not understand their importance. *Chevrolet Celebrity Eurosport, Triphammer, Podkomiter, flies dead on windowsills, C.J., C.J.*

He whispered it. "C.J." It had a comforting sound. It meant something. It was a secret. It had power.

He saw a woman nearby.

He was in the thickest part of the forest, where the trees were closely packed and the foliage overhead formed a barrier nearly impervious to sunlight.

He was sitting up against the trunk of a tree.

And a woman stood nearby.

Naked woman, he could see.

Smiling naked woman with yellow eyes. All breasts and nakedness.

He watched her watch him in the near-darkness.

He smelled her and loved her smell. Despised it. He did not know why.

"I . . . you . . . who . . ." He said. Simple words eluded him.

The woman stared at him, smiled at him, her mouth wide in a hideous lopsided grin. She whispered, "Poor weak child." She smiled as she spoke, yellow eyes wide. "Here you are. Forever. *That* is my power."

"Power," he said.

Marie! he thought. She was a mist, a thing with his mother's face, a thing that suffocated, a moving point of light in the darkness.

He smelled her.

He had always enjoyed her smell, and then, because he hated her, had hated her smell.

"Christopher Jonathan, I am here," she whispered.

Christopher Jonathan, he wondered. It was a secret. It had power.

"Here you are," she said. "Forever."

"Forever," he said.

She said, "I tame the winds, I ride the winds!"

"Bullshit," he said.

"Brat!" she screeched. She had misunderstood him. She misunderstood much.

"Bullshit," he said.

Marie, Aaron, Celebrity Eurosport, Triphammer, Podkomiter, Antlers Drive, flies on the windowsill, bullshit—the words and images of his life flitted about randomly in his head.

The forest was darker than it should have been, given the hour. The storm had taken the light away. The trees were like ghosts. The air was a dark mist.

"Bullshit!" he said, then said it again, and again, and again.

The woman advanced on him.

Celebrity Eurosport, Triphammer, stinging nettle, Antlers Drive—the words and images of his life flitted about randomly in his head, like insects in the dark.

FORTY-ONE

The body breathed. It needed no memory or history for that (picnics on spring afternoons; love on cold mornings; pancakes and real maple syrup; puzzling over bones six thousand years old). The body inhaled, exhaled, inhaled.

Goose bumps rose on it from the cool air brought in by the storm.

The eyes, half open, blinked now and again as a purely involuntary reaction to the drying of the eyeballs (grief, more intense and real than physical pain; lingering at a graveside and whispering good-byes).

The heart beat, the blood circulated, respiration happened—all as it had in the womb, when memories had yet to form, when the body was merely a living set of potentialities (growing up and falling in love; finding a career; buying a home; having children).

The body did not react aloud to pain. Messages of pain flashed along the synapses to the brain, and the brain accepted these messages, but it did not process them in a way that provided for an "Ouch!" or a scream, or for weeping, or flight.

So, when the storm came and the body was pelted by twigs and pine needles and other forest debris, the body did not react except to the extent that a leg jerked, an arm twitched, the stomach muscles tightened briefly.

The *stuff* that the body was made of—the atoms and molecules which, in various combinations, formed the body's DNA, its tissues, organs, spinal cord, bone marrow, blood, gastric juices—had existed since the beginning of time. So the body survived in an era that was not its own. But the memory structure—the events, faces, names, moments, places—that were necessary to the body's identity did not yet exist and, consequently, had no reality outside the brain itself (Joanna, University, Antlers Drive, Chevrolet Celebrity Eurosport). And so, it had no reality.

Thus, the memories had faded and the brain was being emptied (Josh, coffee, pancakes, CN Tower).

And the body and the brain were readying themselves for a new existence.

The body, lean and white and tall, was physically mature.

But the brain was nearing its infancy.

And it was growing very hungry.

Lorraine did not look at Miles anymore. She cradled his body against hers and whispered that she loved him, and she pleaded with him to stay. But she could not look at him because when she did he took her breath away, and she grew frightened.

C.J. said aloud, "Mama, are you down there?"

The words meant little to him. "Mama" meant—*smile, embrace, a kiss*. The rest of the sentence meant nothing.

He repeated it; "Mama, are you down there?"

And again. "Mama, are you down there?"

He said it a hundred times, two hundred times.

And, at last, "Mama" meant nothing to him, and he

started on a new phrase that he pulled from the swirling, debris-laden mists that comprised what had once been his incredible memory.

Aaron remembered it all.

He remembered the car door opening, remembered C.J. looking back, remembered his mother reaching in and pulling him out, remembered the trees, the wind.

Everything.

He was a creature of two worlds, two eras, and so he did not suffer the slow dissolution of memory that his father and his brother were suffering.

He remembered everything.

And he was whole.

This grinning, dark man holding him out for the others to see was a man he had seen before, but only at a distance.

Six years ago.

The man had been looking on, with the others, while Marie had given birth. To him. Aaron.

In a time that she had claimed as her own.

Among these simple people.

She had been mocking them, laughing at them with the fact of his birth.

Aaron remembered it all.

Squealing his first breath. Hearing noises of confusion and anger and fear from all around.

Seeing faces—like the face of this man—turn away, as if in horror.

And now, their faces were turned away again, though the man was smiling, coaxing them—in words whose meaning eluded Aaron, but whose tone was clear—to forget their fear and look.

This is only an ordinary boy. No demon. He squirms the

way rabbits do; he grimaces, lashes out, fights back the way
children do.

Look! You have nothing to fear!

But the others did not look.

They remembered only too well the man they had just
hours before carried to his grave on the island. Remembered only too clearly the dozen others that the screaming
death had claimed in the last two months.

They did not dare look.

This chuckling man, this man who had always been
strange to them, was committing suicide. So be it. The tribe
would be better off without him.

And better off still without this child.

The first stone was cast by a boy of twelve who chanced
a very quick look in the direction of Aaron and the chuckling man, then bent over, found a stone the size of a straw-
berry, and, without looking, heaved it.

The stone fell to earth several yards from where the
chuckling man held Aaron from his outstretched arms.

The chuckling man glanced at the fallen stone and his
smile vanished.

Aaron squirmed in the man's strong grip and pummeled
the man's immense forearms with his tiny fists.

And then the next stone came silently through the air. It
hit the man below the knee. A small *Urp!* of pain started in
the man's throat; he fought it back, made his face blank.

No! he shouted at them. *You fools!*

More stones came, flung blindly.

The man continued to hold Aaron out to his people.
Stones hit the earth around him. Some hit him—on the
thigh, the forehead, the back of his hand. They were not
thrown with much force; they were lobbed, so they caused
the man no great pain.

Fools! he shouted at them. His voice was strong, low, full of authority. *Stop this now!* he shouted. *This is no way to deal with a strange situation!*

But the stones kept coming.

The boy of twelve who had thrown the first one chanced another look at Aaron and the chuckling man. He looked longer this time, and was able to gauge the distance better. So when he threw again, it was with much greater force and accuracy, and the stone, pear-sized, caught the man's temple a glancing blow. The man went down almost immediately on one knee.

He still held Aaron out for his people to see. But Aaron's kicking feet were closer to the ground now and he was able to kick dirt into the man's eyes. In a purely reflexive gesture, the man let Aaron go.

Aaron fell.

A stone hit him on the back of the head and he cried out and grabbed the back of his head.

The stone-throwing stopped at once. A cry of pain from this demon-child was very strange, and unexpected.

Some of the people looked.

They saw Aaron writhing on the ground, hand to the back of his head, eyes closed tightly from the pain.

They saw that the chuckling man was trying to rub dirt from his eyes with one hand and—moving forward with one knee on the ground and the other leg bent—was trying to reach blindly for Aaron with the other.

And they saw that Marie stood behind him.

She had been summoned by the wail of her child in pain.

And she was very angry.

She stepped forward. She grabbed the chuckling man's long, coarse brown hair in one hand, and put the other around the man's chin.

He stiffened.

Who are you? he screamed.

She jerked his head to the right, then to the left, and to the right again.

He was dead.

She let him go.

He fell face-forward, so his body straddled Aaron.

Aaron gasped. He pushed blindly at the dead man, grabbed his hair, pulled it, screamed incoherently, grabbed the dead man's leather garment.

Pulled.

Pushed.

Marie bent over her son and the chuckling man.

The people looking on turned away.

Some ran.

Aaron grabbed blindly; he couldn't breathe under the man's weight.

He grabbed the chuckling man's ax.

Marie pushed the chuckling man's body easily to one side, stooped, lifted her son, crooned, "My boy, my son, my—"

She did not finish the sentence.

The chuckling man's ax caught her hard, and gouged out several square inches of skull.

She crumpled to her knees.

She pitched back.

Her arms went wide, her mouth lolled open and her yellow eyes rolled in their sockets.

Aaron fell with her.

He lay silently for a time.

He felt her body go still under him.

He felt it grow cold.

And then he heard a voice. "My God. Do you think he's all right?"

FORTY-TWO

Lorraine noticed first that Miles was warm again. It took her a while to notice this. For many minutes she had been holding him, had felt his body move rhythmically as he breathed. And his skin had been as cold as the skin of a carrot.

But now it was warm. And she thought that it had probably been warm for quite a while.

She looked at his face. His eyes still were open and staring, but his face was no longer so transparent that it showed her the eye sockets beneath, the cheekbones, the hard rictus grin. It was the face of Miles Gale, and it was whole. Complete. Opaque.

"Miles?" she whispered hopefully.

He moved his head a little so his gaze was on her.

"Miles?" she repeated.

"Uh—" he said.

Lorraine smiled in disbelief and began to weep. He had come back! Miles had come back to her!

"Oh, thank you, Miles," she whispered.

"Demon," Miles said, but the word was unclear coming from his lips and Lorraine thought that he'd said "Darling."

"Darling," she cooed at him. "Darling." And she bent

over and kissed him very lightly and delicately on the cheek, as if he might break if she kissed him too hard.

"Demon," Miles said. "Demon!"

"Darling," Lorraine said.

There was a moment's silence, and Lorraine repeated, "Darling," as she stroked Miles's cheek.

"Darling," Miles said. Then his eyes closed because he was very, very tired.

And he slept.

At Triphammer Mall, a stocky man in a tight blue suit was explaining breathlessly to passersby that the boy he was holding in his arms, "Just appeared here, out of nowhere, out of the air, it's true, I saw it happen!" and Aaron was looking at the stocky man holding him and he was wondering who the man was, and why the man—who was fond of cheap aftershave—smelled like flowers.

And nearby, a woman who had seen what the stocky man had seen, said again, as she had only seconds before, "Do you think he's all right?" and added, "Put my coat on him; he'll catch his death," and she took her gray wool coat off and draped it over Aaron, who looked confusedly at her, at her short red hair and blue eyes and said, "Mama?" and the woman smiled sadly at him and said, "No, dear, oh I'm sorry, no, I'm not your mama."

Then other passersby stopped and questions and suggestions flew everywhere—"Call the security people," and "Was he hit by a car?" and "Does anyone know his name?" and "For God's sake, where are his parents?"

While nearby, just at the edge of the crowd, a tall, thin woman with blond hair and round, golden eyes looked on smilingly—a flat smile full of pleasure and anticipation—and when Aaron cast his gaze from one face to another among the small crowd around him and the stocky man who was holding him, he saw her looking, his eyes grew wide, and he cried happily, "Mama!"

And the red-haired woman who had given him her coat said again, "Oh, dear, no, I'm not your mama, I'm sorry, I'm not your mama."

And a wind started all at once, like a sneeze, and it tossed hats off heads, and made people bend over, and made people scream—because it was so sudden and so strong—and the stocky man holding Aaron knelt down to shelter him from it.

Then the wind was finished.

And when Aaron looked, there was only air where the tall woman with the blond hair and golden eyes had been.

And he began to cry because his mother had been taken from him yet again.

FORTY-THREE

Nine Months Later

Lorraine had planted a row of two dozen sunflowers along the front edge of the yard and they had grown very tall, as tall as a camel's eye, and bees milled about them in a buzzing, yellow profusion. Birds came to the sunflowers, too. Crows, and bluejays especially, and their droppings turned the blacktop road just in front of the yard a smeary gray.

She had gotten complaints about the sunflowers from a few of the neighbors. Peter Harvey said they were an affront to the neighborhood: "No one else has sunflowers," he told her. "They're too . . . big." She asked him if that was his only objection, that they were too big, and he sputtered that a neighborhood should be a place that does not "shock the eye, like those damned sunflowers." She told him she thought they were beautiful, to which he merely huffed and went back home.

This day, the first week of September, the sunflowers drooped from their own weight. Two had actually fallen over and their stiff green stalks lay untidily on the blacktop.

Lisa Brown loved the sunflowers. She had marveled at

the speed at which they grew. And she said now, this first
week in September, that they were proof positive that the
earth was "mother to us all if she can produce something so
wondrous in so short a time." Then, with a nod toward the
house, she asked, "How is Miles doing? Is he making prog-
ress?"

It was a question that Lorraine had grown used to from
her. She had told Lisa time and time again that Miles was
not ill. Not physically, not mentally. He was, in fact, in the
peak of health.

Lorraine said, "He's progressing well."

Lisa nodded. "Up to the McGuffy Reader, is he?"

Lorraine sighed. "We're not using that, Lisa. You know
we're not using that."

Lisa looked suspiciously at Lorraine, as if uncertain that
what the woman was saying was the truth or some feeble
attempt at a joke. Lisa said, "*I* used the McGuffy Reader
with my own preschoolers. It's as good as anything."

"It's ancient, Lisa."

"Oh, for God's sake," Lisa retorted, "we're *all* ancient,
under the skin!"

Aaron came running toward them from the area of the
garage. He was whooping, clapping his open hand to his
mouth, trying to sound like an Indian, but his voice was too
high, and he was smiling besides. He carried a homemade
bow in one hand—the bowstring was a heavy rubber band
doubled over—and a homemade arrow, *sans* point or feath-
ers, in the other.

Lorraine hollered after him, "Warriors don't smile like
that, Aaron."

"Whoo, whoo, whoo!" he answered, sounding more like
a teakettle than a warrior.

A stone-faced C.J. followed him at a loping, unenthusiastic run, as if *play* were a juvenile chore that he was duty bound to attend to. When he passed Lisa and Lorraine, Lisa said, "Hello, C.J., how are you feeling?" but C.J. only nodded at her in a gentlemanly way as he passed.

Lorraine said, "He's awfully sullen these days. Can't blame him. I think Aaron's good for him. They're always together. Aaron will draw him out, eventually; I'm sure of it."

Lisa asked, "C.J.'s still seeing what's-her-name? Dr. French?"

"The social worker? Yes. He'll see her for another six months or so. Then, if we don't get any answers, we'll think about a psychiatrist—someone who can unlock everything, at any rate."

A crow yammered at them from its perch atop the tallest sunflower.

Lisa glanced at it uncertainly; she didn't know what she thought of crows. They were a very forward sort of bird. In her estimation, birds should not be forward kinds of creatures, should not draw too much attention to themselves.

"Let's go inside," Lorraine said.

"I've seen that crow before," Lisa said. "Haven't I seen that crow before? It's very big, isn't it?"

"Who can tell one crow from another?" Lorraine said.

And they went inside to visit Miles.

"Uh-hello," he said, and smiled. The smile was not as vacant as it had been in the past month. There was a trace of the old amusement in it.

Lisa was shocked by it. It seemed so healthy, so real. She tried to smile back, but managed only to make her lips quiver, which made her feel like an ass.

Miles was seated at the kitchen table and he was drinking

what looked like vegetable broth. It was a reddish-orange liquid in a large cream-colored mug.

He was wearing a blue polo shirt and gray pants. His feet were bare. ("He likes to keep his feet bare," Lorraine had said when Lisa had first come over, a week after Miles's recovery. "He likes to flex his toes, you know. I've seen him do it. He seems to get great pleasure from it, from flexing his toes.")

Lisa said now, "Hello, Miles."

"Hello," Miles said, and pushed his chair away from the table, stood, offered Lisa his hand. She shook it quickly, smiled again, said "Hello" once more.

"Have you seen the sunflowers?" Miles asked.

Lisa nodded. "Yes," she answered uneasily.

"Great tall things, and very impressive," said Miles.

"Yes, they're very startling," Lisa said.

"Startling," said Miles. "And there is one crow in particular that seems to enjoy them and is here quite often."

"Yes," said Lisa. "I saw it."

Miles sat down and gestured obligingly at the chair opposite him at the table. "Sit down, why don't you? Have some of this broth."

Lisa shook her head at once. "No. Thank you. I ate."

"What you will, then," he said.

He was seated at a window that overlooked the side yard. Aaron and C.J. were visible through this window. Aaron was still running about, whooping it up. C.J. still plodded after him.

Miles watched them for a moment, then cocked his head and looked at Lisa, then at Lorraine. His face was alive with confusion, but he said nothing. He drank some of his broth by bringing the mug to his lips and sipping delicately.

He set the mug down.

Lisa said, "You're reading well, Miles?"

He smiled at her. There was broth on his mouth and Lorraine pointed at her own mouth discreetly, then at his. He wiped the broth away with a napkin and set the napkin down.

From outside, Aaron let out with a particularly convincing war whoop as he passed close by the kitchen window. Moments later, C.J. appeared, stone-faced, following at a respectful distance.

"Lisa," Miles said, "I think there is a demon in the house."